I0524071

Fugue

Lyn Duclos

Fugue was originally written as a movie-length screenplay when Lyn was
studying her Diploma of Arts (Professional Writing & Editing).
She has since adapted the script into this novel.
Another book, her fourth, is in the research stages and
she's looking forward to beginning the writing soon.
Meanwhile, Lyn's interest in family history, art, music,
theatre, technology and travel, all keep her busy.
Readers can find more information about her other books at:
www.lynduclos.com.au
& on Facebook at: www.facebook.com/lynduclos.author

Fugue

a novel

by

Lyn Duclos

PilandPress

First published by Piland Press
Melbourne, Australia 2016
2/11 Fowler Street, Chelsea, Victoria 3196, Australia
www.lynduclos.com.au

Copyright © Lyn Duclos 2016

All rights reserved. No part of this book may be reproduced or transmitted in any form or by any means, electronic or mechanical, including photocopying, recording or by any information storage and retrieval system, without prior permission in writing from the writer.

National Library of Australia
Cataloguing-in-Publication entry

Creator: Duclos, Lyn, author.

Title: Fugue / Lyn Duclos.

ISBN: 9780975780466 (paperback)

Subjects: Romance fiction.
Melbourne (Vic.)--Fiction.

Dewey Number: A823.4

The characters and events in this book are fictitious and
any resemblance to real persons, living or dead, is purely coincidental.

Printed by Ingram (Worldwide)
November 2016

Cover design by Zozie Brown
Author photo by Pilar Duclos Vargas
Typeset in 11.5 pt Palatino Linotype

Also by Lyn Duclos

SHATTERED REFLECTIONS

WHILE I CAN STILL REMEMBER

Acknowledgements

Dr Janet Mason, MAPS (Consultant Psychologist, Melbourne), always for
her sage advice.

Sandra Tunley (PhD), Counsellor & Psychotherapist, who read the manuscript and provided useful feedback.

Stella Massey, former Musical Director & Conductor of the Cairns Concert
Orchestra, who advised about the technicalities of the music world.

Zozie Brown for her amazing cover illustration. Thank you for your gen-
erosity, both in time and creativity.

Aaron Wood, once again, for helping me with all things tech. I can't begin
to express my gratitude for your time and expertise.

Desirée Duclos, many thanks for always being there for advice on my
website and other related issues. What would I do without you?

My wonderful cousins and friends who read the manuscript and gave me
their opinions, warts and all, along with their tireless efforts on my be-
half: Gail Harber, Genevieve Koenig, Janine Wood, Maria Capannari,
Noreen Owens, Roger Stanley and Tricia Miles.

My beautiful mother, Rosalie Lillian (née Schultz) Mulder, who, due to
Alzheimer's, can no longer read my books, but was such an enthusiast
of this story from the beginning.

My beloved son, Andrés Duclos Vargas, who never had the chance to read
the finished work but always encouraged me in the writing of it.

My treasured daughter, Pilar Duclos Vargas, who read the manuscript
when it was a screenplay and acted it out to time the background music
– no small task! Of course, she's read the manuscript a number of times
and I always value her feedback.

fugue

1 a : a musical composition in which one or two themes are repeated or imitated by successively entering voices and contrapuntally developed in a continuous interweaving of the voice parts
b : something that resembles a fugue especially in interweaving repetitive elements
2 : a disturbed state of consciousness in which the one affected seems to perform acts in full awareness but upon recovery cannot recollect the acts performed

fugue *verb*
fuguist \ ˈfyü-gist\ *noun*

Origin and Etymology of *fugue*
probably from Italian *fuga* flight, fugue, from Latin, flight, from *fugere*
First Known Use: 1597

"Fugue." Merriam-Webster.com. Merriam-Webster, n.d.
Web. 28 Aug. 2016.

For my beloved daughter,

Pilar Duclos Vargas,

whether near or far,

always in my heart and soul.

Prologue

It was dawn. The young sparrow's wing unfolded; her head resumed its alert jerking in every direction of possible danger. The
first rays of a weak sun faintly framed the leaves of the trees that
held the bird and her companions. A snapped twig set her off
her perch in fright, twittering nervously as she flapped vigorously into the air and over the canopy. Here the view of the city
was unimpeded. The sparrow climbed higher, revelling in the
freedom of flight and the wind streaming through her feathers.

She saw the movement of the treetops below as if they were
beckoning. She circled, watching, wary of the frantic patterns the
branches made in the gathering wind. Clouds scurried from the
west towards the city. They held rain and thunder. She looked to
find shelter again with others of her kind. As she reached the
canopy, she levelled off until she found the ideal opening
through the branches.

A sudden flash of lightning startled the sparrow and a clap of
thunder sent her reeling to the ground where she lay, heart beating faster than the steady thrum of heavy rain that bounced off
leaves, branches and earth. Unable to move as she gathered
strength, the sparrow's eyes swivelled frantically around.
Branches leaned inwards, curving towards the ground. The tree
roots seemed to lift out of the earth, threatening to roll her over
and bury her. Thunder roared and rumbled as it stabbed bolts of
lightning through the clouds. Wind tore at the trees and shrubs
and tossed the sparrow hard between the fig tree's roots. She lay
there, twice stunned, resting on a layer of rotted wet leaves.

Her heart pumped strongly, surging the blood through her
tiny veins. The first flutter jerked her body and feeling came back
to bring renewed life and survival. Her beak burrowed tentatively into a damaged wing—but not so damaged that flight was

"

impossible. She took flight—joined with severed leaves and twigs and petals—to reach a sheltering tree where other sparrows huddled close in a cavity.

The storm passed over. Sunlight laughed at the black clouds now dumping their fury over the bay. The sound of dripping, running, gurgling water filled the park. The sparrows shook the water from their wings and swooped down to look for breakfast.

The first morning tram ambled along its metal tracks, and the city heaved itself out of its slumber to begin another day.

Chapter 1

The morning traffic was heavy with Melbourne's workers hurrying to their places of employment. Exhaust fumes already tainted the fresh aroma of the Fitzroy Garden's eucalypts, pines and elms that had been washed clean of the previous day's pollution. The sun, now unimpeded by storm clouds, began its work of persuading flower petals to unfurl in homage to it and to absorb its warmth.

The sparrow watched as a crow unearthed a long fat worm and fly with its prize to a nearby branch where it could enjoy its morning meal. The craving for food had the sparrow flit from branch to branch, eyes ever alert for any telltale signs of movement; an insect, a worm, a discarded crumb or two. There! A human hand swung backwards and something flew out behind it. The something landed on a doorstep in Clarendon Street. The sparrow's head twitched in all directions and, when she perceived no imminent danger, she swooped over car roofs to land beside the prize. It was the remainder of a toasted sandwich. The outer surface was as hard as the crusts, but the sparrow's beak burrowed into the softer interior to taste a mixture of bread, cheese, butter and ham. Her beak darted in and out, taking as much as it could in the shortest space of time, the butter leaving a greasy coating to be cleaned later.

A door opened and a high-heeled shoe emerged onto the step, a hand's breadth from the sparrow and her meal. The bird twittered in alarm and darted out into the traffic, a thundering bus narrowly missing her as she swooped upwards to safety.

Frances Draper closed the shop door and stepped out into the street. She clutched the *Apartments for Sale* section of a newspaper; some of the advertisements were circled in red. She consulted her watch and grimaced with annoyance as she negotiated her way past a group of slow-walking pedestrians. The cut of her tailored suit followed the lines of her slender body as she moved gracefully along the footpath. Her dark hair shone natural mahogany-red lights in the sunlight; it was cut in a free-swinging short bob that complemented her oval face. She wore very little make-up—soft eye shadow that accentuated dark brown eyes, mascara, neutral-toned lipstick. Her jewellery was sparse but expensive; accessories matched.

Her movements were quick, light, purposeful as she neared her car. *One minute to spare*, she thought with relief as she looked at the time left on the parking meter. Not for the first time, she wondered why she bothered owning a car when she had to keep dashing outside to move it so that she wouldn't get booked. With an inward groan, she reminded herself that she had two parking fines overdue for payment—and they were only some of the many she'd received that year.

"There you are!" A man of about thirty years straightened from leaning on the bonnet of his bright red sedan. "I thought you were going to stand me up."

"Sorry," Frances replied as she stepped out of her car. "Caught up in the shop."

"You business women, always busy busy eh?"

He held out his hand to help her up the steps of the building they were about to enter. She avoided him and walked ahead without answering, affording him the opportunity to appreciate the shape of her legs and hips as she moved.

He coughed as he threw his cigarette butt on the pathway and ground it out with his shoe. "You're going to love this one," he enthused as he caught up with her at the doorway.

"I hope so." Her mouth was firm, her expression unimpressed.

"Good security," he pointed out as he opened the door with a key. "See the intercoms in the panel here? You can't get in without someone pushing you in," he laughed at his own joke, "pushing you in…get it?" Frances ignored him. "Pushing the button to let you in," he continued. "Or a key like this one."

"Standard," Frances mumbled.

He coughed again as he led her to the lifts. "Tenth floor. Good position. Large living area, as I said on the phone."

Frances moved away from him in the lift, staring straight ahead of her. It climbed smoothly to the tenth floor. The door opened silently.

"This way, Frances," he said, leading the way.

"Miss Draper."

"Oh." *Up herself,* he thought.

They entered an empty apartment where a dark entrance smelt musty. Frances's lip curled slightly as she pointed wordlessly at peeling paint.

"Oh, they'll fix that up in no time," he assured her.

She moved quickly from room to room, opening and closing doors, then stopped at the lounge room window.

"I thought you said this had a view," she said grimly. The window faced onto the wall of another building.

"The bedroom…" he said weakly.

"The bedroom looks onto train tracks. I'd hardly call that a view."

"Yes, but the price…"

"I told you when we spoke on the phone, Mr…?"

"Mahoney. Ron Mahoney."

"Mr Mahoney. I told you that I want something with a tranquil view—a park perhaps. I want something in good condition— fairly new. A good neighbourhood. Quiet."

"Yes, but…"

"Don't waste my time. If you don't have anything better than this, I'll try another agency."

"No, really, Miss Draper." Ron coughed nervously and smoothed his hair back from his ears. "Those other two apartments. They're much better."

Frances was already walking towards the door.

"I've got forty-five minutes, Mr Mahoney."

"They're both in the same street," he assured her. "We could fit them in, no probs."

Frances inspected the kitchen of the next apartment. The oven door had a broken handle and the inside of it was filthy. She turned to the agent with her eyebrow raised.

"They must have missed that," he said weakly. "Of course they'd have it cleaned and fixed good as new."

"Of course," she replied dryly. "Let's see the other apartment."

"You haven't seen the rest of this one!"

"I don't need to."

The laundry of the last apartment was so small that Frances declined Ron's invitation to enter it with him.

"Where would I put a washing machine?" she asked him.

"The bathroom? It's a huge one."

"I don't think so."

He followed her into the kitchen where she was looking out of the window.

"Nice view," he said, moving close beside her. "You wanted a park."

"Yes, it is nice," she admitted. She could smell his nervous sweat and moved away from him. "But there's nothing on the other side of the building. I want a park on my lounge room side. I can hardly bring all my books in here and read."

She turned and walked out of the apartment.

"Any luck?"

It was Frances's partner, Samuel Tanner, who called out from behind the counter as she entered *The Bookcase*.

"Ghastly," she replied as she made for the back room.

"Never mind, you're bound to find something soon."

Samuel followed her and leaned his stocky frame against the door, his demeanour casual yet poised.

"I hope you're right. I'm tired of looking." She ran a brush through her hair and checked her reflection in a small mirror on a wall. Her gaze did not include vanity.

"Maybe you're too fussy?"

"Maybe," she admitted. "But if I've got to move, I want to find something that I'm going to be happy in...especially after the trouble I've had where I am now."

"I know. All those wild parties are getting you down. You looked haggard..."

"Stinker," she grinned, throwing her paper at him.

"And all these excursions out with estate agents—I think you've really got a secret lover—but you go off gallivanting, leaving me to deal with a thousand customers while you enjoy yourself..."

"You've guessed my secret!"

Frances gave Samuel a quick friendly hug. The faint smell of his aftershave was a pleasant contrast to that of the estate agent's body odour. His eyes smiled down at her, the corners crinkling into the all-familiar crow's feet, whilst his straight eyebrows rose up in question to accentuate the lines across his forehead.

"So, who is he?"

"The stupendous Ronald Mahoney—bearer of eau de noxious cloud upon a layer of nicely nurtured odor *au naturel,* bearer of

gifts including useless apartments and equally useless sugges-
tions..."

"All right, all right, I get the idea," Samuel laughed. "He's,
what...the fifth estate agent you've been to?" At Frances's nod
he continued, "Has he exhausted all of his options?"

"No, he assures me that he's got veritable palaces to show me,
but I don't think I'll bother."

"Oh, give it a go. What've you got to lose?"

Minutes later they were both busy in the shop with a sudden
influx of customers. They worked easily together, consulting
each other when they needed advice.

At thirty-five years, Frances remained unmarried. Not that she
hadn't caught the eye of many a prospective husband—her at-
tractiveness and intelligence being lures that would have captivated most men—but she created an instant glacial wall between
herself and any man if he ever showed the slightest interest. Of
course, to many, this only increased her allure. They would push
harder to pierce the wall of ice and indifference, confident in
their own masculinity that they would be the one to reach the
inner core that surely was crying out for dominance. But none
ever did get any closer than Frances allowed them. Samuel was
the only male that she felt comfortable with, who was no threat
to her, who demanded and expected nothing. And she gave
nothing but her friendship.

Female friends, too, were very few, and most of those with
whom she did allow any form of intimacy felt frustrated by the
lack of depth in their friendship. Discouraged by what they regarded as her distrust of them, and their failed attempts at pair-
ing her off with their male relatives and friends, they soon lost
interest in any contact and left her alone.

The phone rang while Frances was up on a step-ladder handing books down to a customer.

"Good afternoon," Samuel answered the phone. "This is *The Bookcase*. How can I help you?" He listened and then called across to Frances.

"For you, dear."

"Can you take a message please, Samuel?"

She handed another book down to her customer and looked for another. "These are the earlier editions," she said. "But worth having a look at." She led the customer over to a corner of the shop that was furnished with armchairs and low tables decorated with vases of colourful flowers. It was a welcoming, restful place where many a customer took advantage of the opportunity to choose their purchases carefully after looking through them at leisure, under no pressure to buy from the proprietors of the shop. "I'll leave you to go through them," Frances said softly, as her customer settled into a large armchair. "Just let me know if you want any further assistance."

The customer thanked her and Frances walked over to where Samuel stood behind the counter. "Who was it?" she asked him.

"Mister Body Odour himself."

Frances rolled her eyes.

"He sounded very excited," Samuel continued. "He said he's got the perfect place. Just came in. He thinks you'll take it on first glance."

"Oh, he does, does he?"

"You know where it is?"

Frances pulled a face. "The back lots of Dandenong?"

"On the other side of the gardens here."

"What, the Fitzroy Gardens?" She raised an eyebrow in surprise.

"The very same! Great position. And he wants you to meet him there now."

"I can't just flounce out of here at the drop of a hat..."

"Yes you can." Samuel gave her a gentle push. "We're not that busy. Go and flounce on out. It just might be the one."

"Well, all right, but he'd better not be wasting my time again."

Samuel grinned. "I don't think he'd be game."

Chapter 2

"This is better!" Frances exclaimed.

"You really like it?" Ron looked doubtful, wary of her acid tongue.

"Well…" She turned as he flicked a cigarette into his mouth, lighter at the ready. At her disapproving look, he thought better of it and returned the cigarette to its pack.

"It's in a good area," he said quickly, afraid that his attempt at smoking might have him lose the advantage.

"Are you sure the security system works?"

"Absolutely."

"Yes, but…"

"And look at the view!"

Ron steered her towards the outside wall of the lounge room. He unlocked french doors leading out to a wide balcony. From the fifth floor they had an uninterrupted view of the Fitzroy Gardens spread out as far as Wellington Parade from where the distant rattle of trams reached their ears. To the right, along Albert Street, the city's skyscrapers rammed up into the blue spring sky like mighty horsts raised by the earth in a primeval outburst of energy. To the left, past Eades Street, was the Dallas Brooks Hall, offices and restored old buildings, before the intersection with Clarendon Street in which *The Bookcase* was situated. Frances could see the Epworth Freemasons Hospital to the right of the intersection. The lush greens and browns of the gardens were pleasing to the eye, as were the neat, shady, flowered paths where pine, chestnut, gum, palm, elm and Moreton Bay fig trees, as well as fountains and statues, all combined to provide a tranquil place of leisure.

Frances was fascinated by the unaccustomed view of the gardens from that height, her eyes darting from one point to another as she gained her bearings from what she recognised of the area. Ron scrutinized her face in profile, marvelling at how soft and more attractive she looked with her guard down. He wondered what she'd look like naked and the thought excited him. She was suddenly jolted out of the temporary oblivion of her immediate surroundings when she felt the estate agent's hand on her arm. She stiffened and her facial expression tightened into a cold mask.

"The best view you could get anywhere," he said, sensing her delight with the apartment. "And so close to your work, isn't it?"

"There's that about it," she admitted, crossing quickly to the other end of the balcony.

"You'd only have to walk across the park to get to it!"

Her glance touched upon the canopy of the trees across the road and drifted downwards to the thick trunk of a Moreton Bay fig tree. She frowned, then turned back to the lounge room, but hesitated as she touched the frame of the french door.

"The undercover parking's secure," Ron hurried on. "You wouldn't even have to use your car as much. Think of the saving in petrol!"

Frances failed to respond as she turned slowly back to the gardens, looking intently at the trees—more particularly the large fig tree. Ron's voice faded as a sudden fragmented memory burst into her head. An image of twisted fig tree roots flashed through her mind and was gone as abruptly as it had come. She shook her head slightly, as if to brush a fly away and, puzzled, left the balcony, the incident forgotten.

"…but you'll have to act fast, though." Ron's voice broke into her consciousness. "I've got another client interested in it."

Frances looked at him with contempt. "That's the standard line. How about something more original?"

"No, really! He's very keen." Sweat suddenly formed on Ron's forehead and he wiped at it absentmindedly. "He's putting in an offer tonight. You could beat him to it."

"I thought you said I was the first person you've shown this to."

"Oh, I…"

"How long have you been in this job?"

"Four years!"

She raised an eyebrow in mock surprise. "Really?"

Ron paused, wary of the composed woman regarding him steadily. He hated women like this. They made him feel inadequate—not quite the stud he liked to think he was. Although his blustering seemed to fit the job, and most of his clients allowed him to take over and bulldoze them into quick decisions, he instinctively knew that he could easily lose this sale. And, God how he needed it! His car payment was due in a few days, as well as the mortgage payment on his own townhouse, and the travel agency had been on his back to pay for his Europe holiday or he'd lose the booking as well as his deposit. For the hundredth time he reminded himself that he must curb his big spending habits.

His mind raced as he calculated how to get back in her good books. If he went the hard sell, she might back off, but if he acted indifferently she was just as likely to get in a huff and go to the opposition. She liked the apartment. That was obvious, as she'd not found a thing wrong with it. Maybe she was just being herself—a real bitch—and liked to see him squirm. Well, he'd make her squirm instead.

"He's not the only buyer who's interested. Apartments like these don't come up very often."

She walked thoughtfully around the apartment again, returning to the kitchen, the master bedroom, the bathroom. She opened cupboard drawers, looked into the oven, inspected the shower recess. He waited, irritated, wondering if she was deliberately ignoring him. When she returned to the lounge room, she drifted over to the windows overlooking the Fitzroy Gardens. She stood for some moments in silence as she regarded the view.

He fidgeted with the cigarette lighter in his jacket pocket, waiting.

"I don't know…" she said finally, her back to him.

"It fits all your requirements. Everything!"

She turned to face him. "Do you have anything else to show me?"

"Not like this one." He waited as they regarded each other. "It's…you! I can tell," he finished off smugly.

"I hardly think you're in a position to know what is me," she said icily.

"No—I meant…"

Frances laughed. "Look, perhaps I'd better see some others before jumping in on this one."

"What…?"

"Just to make sure." She whirled around, taking in the clean new apartment in one turn. The walls were painted a subdued ivory that would complement her many framed paintings; the pale green carpet was unmarked, the pile deep, and it smelled freshly cleaned; the light fittings gleamed as though new. *This is perfect!*

"What's wrong with…?

She laughed again at his confusion, glad to see the smugness wiped off his face.

"Well," he ground out, "are you interested?" An image of a cat playing with a mouse came to his mind.

"Let's put an offer in and see what happens," she said quietly as she walked out of the apartment.

He sighed, his shoulders sagging with relief. Sweat liberally soaked the shirt underneath his jacket. The craving for a cigarette was unbearable. *The bitch! I hope she drops dead once she moves in. At least I'll have my commission.*

On a sunny spring day five weeks later Frances took possession of the apartment.

The last of the furniture and boxes had been unloaded and she looked around at the disorder hardly knowing where to start. There was no cleaning to do, as every room was spotless. All she had to do was unpack.

"I know what we'll do first, Plato," she said to her cat, carrying him over to her stereo. "We'll set this up and put on a CD and then get you some lunch. What do you say to that, eh?"

Minutes later she had the stereo plugged in and she took a CD from one of the labelled cartons stacked up beside it. Max Bruch's *Concerto No. 1 for Violin and Orchestra in G minor* soon filled the apartment.

"There, that's better," she told Plato. "I hope the neighbours like music."

Plato followed her into the kitchen where she rummaged around in some cartons until she found where she'd packed his food. She filled a bowl for him and put the remainder into the empty fridge, which she turned on at the wall. The motor kicked into life and settled down to a low hum. Turning back to the cartons, she hunted around until she located a bottle of wine.

"I've been saving this shiraz for a special occasion," she said, holding the bottle up to the light. "Well, I think this just about fits in to that category. Now all I have to do is find a glass."

After quite some hours of unpacking, there were just nine more boxes left in the lounge room; she tackled the first.

"Ah, here they are!"

The box contained framed photographs and pictures. The first one she pulled out was a photograph of her parents when they were young. Her father stood playing a violin and her mother was sitting at a piano. His tall figure was clothed in a black tuxedo, the satin lapels shining under the light of a chandelier, black bow tie contrasting with the white dress shirt. Frances's mother wore a dark green strapless satin dress with a full skirt that fanned out over the piano stool. Her hair, piled up in a French roll, gleamed darkly against her porcelain skin. Her lipstick and nail polish were matching blood red. Not for the first time Frances thought the red to be the only sign of life in the scene. She looked at the photograph for a long moment, memories flooding back of the parents she hardly knew. The concentrated expression on her father's handsome face held a passion and surrender to the music that she had only seen when he played the violin or watched his wife play. It was not an expression that ever included his daughter. She sighed, then walked around the room with the photograph until she found a place for it upon a side table.

The next frame she took from the box was a close-up of Samuel. She smiled at it fondly, her eyes taking in his greying sandy hair combed back neatly from his wide forehead. She remembered the occasion when the photograph was taken—it was at an opening of an exhibition of a young artist twelve months prior. It had been a formal occasion and Samuel looked the part in his dinner jacket and black bow tie. She could just make out the blurred figures of other patrons of the gallery behind him. He was smiling at the camera; it was a smile reaching from his generous mouth to his blue-grey eyes that held a genuine warmth in their expression.

"Samuel, dear, you will go here," Frances said aloud as she placed the photograph upon an antique secretaire. She stood back to admire it. "Yes, perfect!"

The rest of the pictures she hung on the walls, reluctantly hammering nails into the clean-painted surface, and then she opened another box. A bust of Beethoven took pride of place on a shelf of a wall unit, to be surrounded by other objets d'art that were the fruits of Frances's occasional holidays away from Australia. Amongst them were a carved malachite Mayan calendar, which she placed upon a stand; and a petite bust of Nefertiti, carved smoothly from alabaster.

Thoughts of a proposed overseas trip crowded her mind as she regarded her souvenirs. Samuel had suggested they travel together to Europe sometime in the near future, if they could find a trustworthy manager to take care of *The Bookcase*, but so far they had had no success in finding one.

The rest of the boxes held the contents of the secretaire and many books that revealed her taste in fiction, non-fiction—including large books on art, music, composers, and the like. She handled them with the utmost care, rediscovering them as precious old friends.

She worked on, shelving the books, stopping from time to time to look out at the gardens below as if irresistibly drawn by a magnetic force. Each time she paused at the french doors a thoughtful expression filled her eyes. The tree branches with their full, heavy, summer coating of leaves, swayed in the light breeze. There was a thought, a memory, tickling her mind, like a word that fails to reach the tip of the tongue—maddening in its elusiveness.

Plato rubbed against her legs. She picked him up and stroked his soft jet-black fur. His emerald green eyes regarded her with adoration.

"What do you think of your new home?" she asked him. "I think we'll like it here." He licked her hand as if in agreement.

They both turned towards the front door when they heard the ring of the security buzzer.

"Hello?" she said into the speaker of the intercom.

"It's me. Samuel."

"Oh, Samuel! How nice. Come on up."

She pushed the button and heard the downstairs door click open.

"Our first visitor, Plato."

Frances opened the door to Samuel, who, with a flourish, handed her a bunch of yellow roses.

"Yellow for friendship and joy," he said as she offered her cheek to him.

"How sweet! You are a dear, Samuel. Always so thoughtful."

He walked into the apartment, looking around him with interest. "How's the unpacking going?"

"Nearly finished." She went into the kitchen with the roses and took a vase out of a cupboard. "Would you like a coffee?"

"No. No. I'm on my way out. Just thought I'd have a quick tour."

They walked around the apartment and then went out on the balcony. "You didn't exaggerate," Samuel commented. "Marvellous view you've got." He leaned over the railing. "Have you met any of the neighbours yet?"

"Just the couple who live on the floor below me."

"Nice?"

"Seem to be."

"Anyone else?"

She shook her head. "No." A sparrow landed on the railing at the opposite end of the balcony. It hopped along the railing towards them but when Frances reached out slowly towards it, it flew away.

"You'll have them eating out of your hand soon," Samuel smiled.

"I hope so," she said. "Oh, it's so peaceful here, despite the traffic. So much greenery!"

"Quite a contrast to your old place, eh?"

"My goodness, yes! I think Plato and I are going to be very happy in our new home."

"It took you long enough to find it."

"It had to be just right. I don't want to have to move again—ever."

Chapter 3

At eight-thirty the next morning, Frances closed the security door behind her. It clicked shut as she descended the stairs and made her way along the footpath on Albert Street. Her short-sleeved lemon dress hugged her figure as a warm summer breeze played around it. Leather high-heeled sandals matched the small black handbag that she carried over her left arm. Thick square gold earrings echoed the shape of a gold pendant that hung over the edge of her neckline. Her hair, gleaming healthy mahogany lights in the sunlight, was tucked loosely behind her ears. Hers was a figure that drew the attention of many a male eye.

Entering the gardens, she took a path that led left through a wide expanse of trees. The faint sound of running water reached her ears over the traffic and she turned to find the River God fountain through an arch formed by the branches of a large Moreton Bay fig tree. Her attention was drawn away from the fountain momentarily as she walked past the tree, stopping to look at its formation. Inexplicably, a feeling of uneasiness swept over her, but the fountain claimed her again and she shrugged off the feeling. The concrete figure of a man on bended knee, holding an open clam shell on his shoulders, formed the central feature of the fountain with water falling around him from the shell above. She smiled, thinking what beautiful surroundings she had to enjoy so close to her new home.

The path branched off to her right and she strolled along it, passing another fountain set back behind a long row of trees. Further along, she passed a model Tudor Village and a Fairy Tree—features which she already knew were there, but had never had the time or the inclination to explore. She promised herself to have a good look at them on her way home from work that evening.

Turning left, another path led straight towards Clarendon Street. The path was lined with flowers and trees, varicoloured greens contributing a peaceful and relaxing setting for the people who were fortunate enough to be able to enjoy the gardens. A mere five steps up to street level and she passed between two statues—one of a mermaid and a fish, and the other, a boy and a pelican.

How little notice I've taken of all this beauty, she chided herself with a backward glance as she waited for an opening in the traffic. She crossed the road and entered *The Bookcase*.

Samuel took an armful of books from a box and read out the titles to Frances as she checked them against a stock list.

"McCullough, Colleen. *Bittersweet*," he said. "A dozen here."

"Right," Frances answered.

The door of *The Bookcase* opened to a young man dressed in a business suit.

"May I help you?" Samuel asked the man, as he put the books down beside Frances.

"Yes, can you show me what you have on harpsichords?"

"Harpsichords? The history of? Players of?"

"Oh—history and making—something like that."

Samuel led the man to the music section of the shop. "What specifically were you after?"

"Well, I'm looking for anything you might have on when the second keyboards were introduced."

"Oh. You've got me stumped. I think we might have to ask the expert over there."

They both turned to Frances whose head was bent over the stock list.

"Frances, dear?"

"Yes?" She looked up at him enquiringly.

"This gentleman would like something on the harpsichord…what was it again?"

"The addition of the second keyboard."

"Oh, yes," Frances said, getting to her feet. "The Germans added them in the late sixteenth century, I think."

The man nodded. "That's right."

"Let's see," Frances mused. "Oh yes." She withdrew a book from a shelf. "Here's something that might help you."

She bent over the book with the man who accidentally bumped her. Almost imperceptibly, she shifted away from him, putting the book between them.

In the next block from *The Bookcase,* Frances entered a small restaurant that had recently opened on the second floor of a Clarendon Street building. Appropriately enough, the restaurant had been named *Parklands* as its windows faced onto a view of the Fitzroy Gardens.

Frances looked around the tables already occupied and saw that her friend, Gail, was already seated at a window table. She smiled to herself as Gail waved frantically at her.

"I thought I'd never get here," Frances exclaimed as she sat down.

"Held up at the shop again?" Gail asked, pushing her unruly hair out of her eyes. The thick, dark waves bounced back of their own accord.

Frances nodded. "I seem to be late nearly every time we arrange to meet. Sorry."

"I wouldn't call five minutes late, Frances. Stop worrying."

"Well, thanks." Frances smiled at Gail who sipped on a glass of iced water. "Don't tell me you've given up smoking *and* drinking!"

Gail pulled a face. "Neither."

"But…"

"I know. I know." Gail held up her hands in surrender. "I lasted five whole weeks this time."

Frances laughed. "That's what…? A week longer than last time?"

"Something like that."

"Impressive."

"Getting better, aren't I?"

"Let's see, at that rate you'll be a non-smoker by the time you reach ninety-nine."

"My lungs are feeling better already!"

Frances looked at her friend affectionately. They'd been friends for ten years, ever since Frances had first attended the dental practice where Gail worked as a young dentist. It had amused Frances greatly how her new dentist had prattled on asking questions through her spotless mask, regardless of the fact that Frances's mouth was full of instruments, making any response impossible. When Gail had learned about Frances's then occupation as a librarian at the State Library, she would conduct a running commentary on the books she was reading at the time, asking Frances what she thought of them. Frances learned to grunt at the appropriate times and was amazed that Gail knew how to interpret the grunts.

Frances found her dentist to be one of the most unaffected persons she knew. Totally unselfconscious, and bubbling over with enthusiasm for anything and everything, Gail took a keen interest in the lives and activities of her patients. She took them to her heart, cared for them, felt for them, agonized with their pain—for which she felt totally responsible, despite the fact that her patients hardly suffered at her hands. Frances often thought about why Gail hadn't become a doctor or a nurse instead because of her nurturing attitude.

"Oh, I'd never be any good at nursing," Gail had laughed when Frances asked her before her mouth was invaded again.

"The thought of changing a bedpan makes me feel like throwing up!"

Frances had smiled to herself, thinking of the dreadful mouths Gail must have come across during her career. She'd wondered if the remains of her last evening's meal, which included garlic prawns, was wafting up from her stomach.

"Garlic's a nice smell," Gail had commented, reading Frances's thoughts. "I eat so much of it myself anyway. Probably make all my patients ill with it!" And she had exploded in a fit of giggles. "Dirty teeth and mouths are easy to clean once I've got them under these," she continued, holding up her rubber-gloved hands. "Give 'em a blast with this…" she squirted the water and then the air, "…and this, and I've got all sorts of lovely smelling antiseptics and so on." She held up an instrument with a fine hooked end. "And the rest I can get off with this, or the drill."

But it was their shared interest in books that had developed their friendship over the years. Gail took to visiting the library to consult Frances about which books she *should* read to improve her mind, as she put it. So Frances steered her through the classics and right through to postmodern writers. When Samuel enticed Frances away from the library to become his partner in *The Bookcase*, Gail went with her as a loyal customer. On many an occasion, she would call in to *The Bookcase* to pick up 'something to fill the book shelves at home'. She would sprawl out in one of the armchairs with a pile of 'possibles' on the table in front of her, and enjoy a coffee while she 'salivated over them'. Samuel enjoyed Gail's infectious personality as much as Frances did, especially when she held court in the *Poet's Corner*, as she had dubbed it, with many a lively discussion erupting amongst a group of customers seated there.

Frances was brought back to the present as Gail reached over and tapped her on the hand.

"You haven't heard a word I've said."

"What…?"

"About joining us for dinner. As I said, it's all arranged."

Frances paused while she pushed some salad greens onto her fork. "No, I'd really rather not."

"It's about time you dragged yourself away from that shop of yours. Have a good time for a change."

"I'm happy in the shop."

"I'm talking about men, Frances. You know—those creatures with hard, muscular bodies who're nice to go out with occasionally."

"I go out with Samuel," she said deliberately, looking up from her plate.

"Samuel!" Gail snorted. "He's a hundred and four!"

"Forty-five to be exact."

"What good's he to you?"

"I enjoy his company. We share a lot of interests."

"So?"

"We've been together for years. You know that."

"Come on, Frances," Gail chided her. "I'm talking about a *real* man." She paused as she took a sip of wine, watching Frances's face carefully. "Like Bob, for instance."

"Bob?" Frances laughed good-naturedly. "Oh, Gail, you're incorrigible."

"No, really." She gesticulated with a piece of bread. "He likes you."

"You've tried to match me up with your brothers—poor fellows—and now your cousins too!"

"Why not go out with Bob? He's lots of fun."

"No. It's pointless."

"No, it's not!"

"It is," Frances said quietly and firmly.

"But why?" Gail insisted. "You're a good looking woman." She looked at Frances critically through a frame made by her fingers. "You've got a lot going for you. It's unnatural."

"What is?" Frances looked up surprised.

"Not having any relationships." Gail ignored Frances's mute protest. "You're thirty-five, for God's sake! Don't you want to have any children?"

There was the slightest hesitation. "Not particularly."

"Well, at least someone to have sex with!"

"No!"

Gail didn't miss the venom in Frances's voice, or her revulsion at the idea, but she pressed on. "I'll bet you and dear old Samuel haven't got that far!"

"Of course not!" She blushed. "Look...I'm not that way inclined."

"Don't you need someone? Anyone?"

Frances played with her glass, running her forefinger around the rim of it, without looking at Gail.

"You're not...you know...queer, are you?"

Frances looked up at her, startled. "What? A lesbian?"

Gail nodded wordlessly, concern written all over her face.

"No, "Frances assured her. "Not at all. I'm just...content the way I am."

"I hope so," Gail replied slowly, unconvinced. "But if you change your mind about Bob..."

"I won't." She looked down at her watch. "Oh, my goodness! I'll be late." Her chair scraped against the floor tiles as she stood suddenly. "I must get back to the shop. Samuel has to go out this afternoon."

"Sure. You go. I'll fix up the bill."

"Thanks." Frances bent over to kiss Gail's cheek. "I'll get it next time."

As she made a quick escape from the restaurant, her friend looked after her with concern. *Stop trying to run her life*, she scolded herself. *She knows what she's doing. I think.*

Not waiting for the lift, Frances hurried down the staircase to the ground floor, then almost ran out of the front door, not looking to her left as she bounded down the stairs to the footpath.

"Oh, I'm so sorry," she exclaimed, bumping into a young woman pushing a pram. "I wasn't looking where I was going."

"That's okay," the woman said. "No harm done." She looked over to the gardens where a young man waved, and then pushed the pram across the road to join him.

Frances hesitated as she saw the couple embrace and kiss lingeringly. The man's arms were around the young woman's body, pulling her close to him, and her arms were around his neck, her hands caressing his hair. *Young love,* Frances smiled to herself, as she unconsciously smothered a tingling sensation in her groin. The couple broke apart and bent over the pram, fussing over the sleeping baby. They exuded togetherness, belonging, love.

A wistful unhappiness scattered through Frances, but she denied it the luxury of an explanation in her mind. She glanced at her watch again, turned on her heel and hastened towards *The Bookcase*.

Chapter 4

Melbourne's Hamer Hall bustled with the arrival of concert go-ers as they made their way to their seats. The atmosphere buzzed with animated conversations, rustling programme pages, the clearing of throats and full-bodied coughs without the fear of a frown of admonishment. On the stage, the members of the orchestra adjusted their chairs to the correct position and fiddled with their sheet music in front of them. An expectant hush descended upon the hall as the door opened and the concertmaster entered the stage. He tuned the orchestra, section by section. The stage door opened again and two men emerged: the conductor and the featured pianist for the evening.

The conductor raised his baton and nodded to the pianist. A single emphatic chord from the full orchestra began Beethoven's *Piano Concerto No. 5* with an opening flourish from the pianist.

Frances and Samuel sat absorbed in the music from their usual seats in the front row of the stalls. Their view of the pianist was unobstructed. They thrilled at the agility and speed of his fingers, his faultless memory that enabled him to play without any music in front of him, and they admired his interpretation of the concerto.

As the pensive brooding of the slow second movement held the audience captive, Frances's breathing deepened as if she were taking the music piece by piece into her body through the pores of her skin. Her eyes glazed as tears filled them and slowly, drop by drop, the tears slid over the edges of her lids and dripped unheeded down her cheeks.

The concerto shifted to the third movement, plunging into a bold transformation until it finished with a dynamic finale. Frances's tears gradually subsided during the movement, and she smiled as she joined the rest of the audience in a rousing appreciation of the pianist's performance. Samuel was unaware of her hand's furtive sweep across her face that left no evidence of her emotion.

It took Samuel some minutes to fight his way back from the bar through the noisy crowd, balancing two glasses of champagne as he did so. He found Frances studying the programme.

"Thanks," she smiled, as she took a glass from him.

"Still reading?" he smiled.

"I don't know how Beethoven did it."

"With a great deal of skill, I would imagine," he nodded, "given his hearing loss."

"Oh, yes," she nodded in agreement, the memory of the concerto still playing in her head.

"To the pianist!" he said, tapping his glass against hers.

"Wasn't he magnificent?"

"Superb!" Samuel agreed. "A faultless performance."

"And did you notice the new violinist?"

"The concertmaster?"

"Yes."

"Wonder where he came from?"

"I read about him somewhere." Frances looked down at the programme in her hand. "What a marvellous selection tonight."

"Umm…what's on after interval again?"

"The short Saint-Saens piece and then the Rachmaninov."

"Oh, that's right." He took a sip of his champagne as his eyes meandered over the crowd. He nodded at someone, then turned back to Frances. "I'm looking forward to the Mozart series next season."

"Yes, there'll be some very talented musicians here for it."

"Like whom?"

"Avan Yu," she replied. "He won the 2012 piano competition in Sydney."

"Oh yes—damned good pianist."

"And that young conductor. What's his name…?

"God, Frances," Samuel grimaced. "I can't remember. That's what I've got you for!"

"Oh, thanks a lot," she pulled a face at him in mock hurt. "Don't you love me for my salubrious company?"

"Never, dear girl. It's just your brain I love."

They wandered through the foyer, glasses in hand, stopping to look at displays of stage memorabilia in glass cabinets, commenting upon various works of art hanging on the walls, and looking at pamphlets set out on tables. Occasionally they encountered people they knew—acquaintances, mostly from business connections—and they separated, chatting from time to time with individuals.

Frances looked for Samuel as the bell rang for the audience to return to the hall for the second half. She noticed him engaged in an animated conversation with a well-dressed man of about his own age. Samuel wrote something on a slip of paper and handed it to the other man. The two men smiled wordlessly at each other for a long moment. The other man touched Samuel lightly on the forearm and then turned to go to his seat. His figure was swallowed up instantly by the crowd but Samuel still looked in his direction. Frances regarded him thoughtfully and smiled to herself as he rejoined her.

"Someone I know?" she asked.

"No," he replied quickly. "Come on." He steered her towards their door.

The Saint-Saens *Introduction & Rondo Capriccioso* was a lively beginning to the second half of the concert. The piece was as familiar to Frances as any of the memories from her childhood—memories of her father and mother and the music they played.

Frances is hiding behind the umbrella stand in the hallway. She peeps between tall white lilies set in a long green vase through to the open lounge room door. The scene is hazy around the edges, blending into the sides of her mental image. Her father stands alone in the middle of the room. He is playing the *Introduction & Rondo Capriccioso.* Small droplets of perspiration appear upon his forehead. Her mother and five other musicians are in the room watching him. Everyone is dressed formally, except for Frances, who looks down at her white cotton nightie in dismay. Her father's gaze leaves his wife's face to stare in the direction of Frances. She shrinks backwards, towards the staircase, afraid she will be discovered. The music finishes and her mother rises to her feet applauding him enthusiastically along with the other musicians.

Frances felt Samuel's shoulder brush against her own as he applauded the new concertmaster. She blinked, clearing her glazed eyes to see the violinist regarding her thoughtfully. Her face was wet with tears and she swept them away, embarrassed, wondering if her tears were visible from the stage.

Chapter 5

The morning traffic was heavy as Frances crossed Albert Street. She thought once again how fortunate she was to have her home and work close enough together so that she could walk between them—and in such pleasant surroundings. Two joggers passed her on the path as she paused at the River God fountain. Birds splashed in the pond beneath it, flapping their wings in a shower of water that reached Frances. She laughed softly, not wanting to frighten them. A sparrow hopped from stone to stone towards her, its head jerking in all directions, but when it saw she had nothing to offer, the bird rejoined its kind.

"Tomorrow I'll bring you some crumbs," she promised. "So you'd better be here on time."

From its perch, the sparrow twittered cheekily as if in answer.

She looked back towards the large fig tree she'd already passed, as if someone had called out to her, but seeing nothing she continued on her way towards *The Bookcase*. A flock of sparrows flew close by and she turned to see if they were the same ones that had been at the fountain. Seeing them gone from the water, her vision swept over the tree; her footsteps slowed and she paused. Retracing her steps, she neared the tree and, looking up through the branches, she stared at the canopy. It began to revolve slowly as the light filtered through it, seemingly drawing her back to the trunk. She walked around the base of it, running her hands along the high walls of the roots that formed twisted corridors snaking towards the trunk. Green fungus partly covered them and she reached out to touch the bark which cracked into small pieces, inviting her fingers to shred them off.

A sudden faltering of her heart, a giddiness, a sense of falling into blackness, swamped her. Where her fingers had been shredding off the bark, now there were a small child's fingers picking at it. She staggered, but regained her balance by holding onto a root wall. A burning sensation pricked the nerve endings of her fingers and she recoiled, startled, then turned and walked quickly away, almost breaking into a run. She gradually forced her breathing back to normal and slowed to a walk. With relief she noticed that no one else in the gardens was close enough to have seen her reaction. She felt stupid, chiding herself, though not sure what for. Her shoulders wriggled into their customary straight position, her chin went up, and her face resumed the cool, impassive disguise that it normally wore.

When Frances reached *The Bookcase* a few minutes later, Samuel had not yet arrived. She had time to settle down and open the shop ready for the day and, by the time he walked in, she had poured boiling water into a coffee plunger and had their mugs at the ready.

"You'd make a good wife for somebody someday," he commented, sniffing the aroma appreciatively.

"Slave, do you mean?"

"Probably."

He took a mug from her and opened his folded newspaper, scanning the front page quickly. She walked over to the front window and looked over at the gardens, cupping her coffee mug between her hands. Samuel raised an eyebrow, asking himself how she could have cold hands on such a warm morning, but decided against commenting. His shirt sleeves were already rolled up—a concession to the warm day predicted—but his neck was firmly encircled by the ever-present tie. He turned his thoughts, instead, to the business at hand.

"Frances, dear, how long before the back orders arrive? Do you remember?"

"Umm...?"

"Do you remember?"

"Remember what?"

"You're not listening to me."

She still had her back to him. "Umm…?"

"Are you all right?" Receiving no response, he watched her for a moment, taking in her slim, well-dressed figure. There was something different about her, he thought, but couldn't quite figure out what. It was in her stature, he decided. Were her shoulders slumped? No. She just didn't look her normal brisk self. He walked over beside her. "Frances?"

"What?" She appeared to be startled out of a trance. "Oh, no," she said turning to face him. "I'm fine, Samuel. Just fine."

"Well, as I was saying," he replied, looking slightly miffed, "about the back orders."

"Yes."

"Well, do you remember?"

"Remember what?"

"You *are* a dreadful trial today!" He frowned at her, then enunciated each word slowly. "Do you remember when the back orders are due in?"

"Of course, dear," she said, wondering why he seemed put out. "Tomorrow afternoon."

"Thank you, mademoiselle!" He paused, looking at her thoughtfully. "You know, you're looking a bit peaky. A weekend at Mother's would do you the world of good."

"Do you think so?" she replied absently.

"Yes I do," he told her sternly. "I'll ring her right now. She'll be pleased to know you're coming with me."

"It may not suit her at such short notice."

"No, it's all right. She said this weekend would be fine."

"What do you mean?" She rounded on him. "Have you already spoken with her?"

"Well, sort of," he admitted.

"Samuel?"

He looked guilty. "She and Dad are forever asking after you. They adore you! You know that."

"You've already arranged it?" Her face looked stiff, cold. "Without asking me first?"

"I was only thinking of you…"

"Apparently," she said a trifle coldly.

"I'm sorry, dear," he said, taking her hand. "I didn't mean to step on your toes. You're probably tired after the big move and I just wanted to give you a rest."

"Yes, I know." She paused as she looked out at the gardens again.

"Well?"

"All right," she turned to smile at him. "I'll go."

"Terrific!"

Samuel dashed over to the counter and picked up the phone before she could change her mind. He pushed a button and waited.

"Hello, Mother?" He listened for a moment. "Yes, she's coming!"

The weekend's weather forecast was promising for Daylesford, which is a little more than an hour's drive north-west from the city. Helen and Howard Tanner lived in a restored weatherboard house near the shores of Lake Daylesford. The house had been their holiday and weekend retreat—doing it up gradually and adding bits of antique furniture as and when they had found them—until ill health had forced Howard to retire, leaving *The Bookcase* in the hands of their son to sell. Samuel had arranged for the sale of their home in Brighton, where he had spent most of his childhood, and he then moved his parents to Daylesford where they had always wanted to be. But when it came to selling *The Bookcase*, Samuel had second thoughts.

Fugue

For most of his life, Samuel had followed a carefully planned, risk-free path charted by his parents. They had provided him with an excellent education in private schools and university, as well as introducing him to society in the 'right circles'. Far from being snobs, they had wanted the best for their only child, and that's what they gave him. After graduating from the University of Melbourne with a Bachelor of Commerce, the proud parents presented their son with a return air ticket to Europe and enough spending money to keep him for a year's sightseeing. He returned exactly twelve months later, after having visited the 'right' countries and seen the 'right' monuments, galleries, concert halls, cathedrals and museums. He was then ready to pursue his chosen career of accounting and, after the obligatory three years service in a chartered accountant's office, he then set up his practice in Toorak. It was one kilometre from his two-bedroomed apartment in South Yarra, towards which his parents put in a sizeable chunk of the purchase price.

Samuel's apartment gradually filled with antique furniture and paintings which he collected and paid for from his substantial earnings. On the evenings that he stayed at home, he prepared complicated and exotic meals for himself, indulging in the arts of cooking and eating, both of which he enjoyed enormously. He frequented the best of restaurants and, inheriting his parents' love of classical music, books and art, was a frequent visitor to galleries and concerts. Not a lover of football, or any of the masculine sports, he played no sport and indulged in very little exercise, other than the occasional walk. His figure, as a result, had, by the time he was in his late thirties, become quite portly in a comfortable sort of way.

Once Samuel had built up his accountancy practice and was financially comfortable in his own right, he became bored with the sameness of each day, week, month, year. He felt restless, unchallenged and unfulfilled. *Surely there's more to life than this,* he had asked himself. When his father became ill and asked

Samuel to sell *The Bookcase*, the idea of taking it over himself appeared as an attractive solution to his problems. *Why not?* he considered. He knew that he was a damned good accountant and, with careful budgeting, he'd get the business back on track in no time. *But I don't know enough about books!* Then he had remembered the attractive librarian at the State Library who had helped him out on many an occasion. *What about her? Would she give up her job to go into partnership with me?* He shook his head. *No, she'll think I'm a madman.*

But he went to the library anyway. He walked straight up to her desk and said, "Miss Draper, you know me." It was a statement, not a question.

"Yes, I know you," she smiled in that quiet, dignified way of hers. "You're Samuel Tanner, the accountant, who tries to flummox me with the most difficult requests of any visitor to the library."

"And you always rise to the occasion and are totally unflummoxed," he replied.

"I try." Her look was amused with a tinge of derision.

He leaned over her desk, his weight on his fingers splayed in a wide web, the manicured fingernails turning white. The pressure between his fingers and the desk disguised any hint of nervousness she might have seen if his hands had been unoccupied. "Do you like your job?" he asked bluntly.

She looked startled. "Yes…of course I do!" She tossed her hair back from her face unconsciously tucking one side behind an ear.

"Ah!" His fingers left the desk. "I sensed a hesitation there."

"Pardon?"

"Hesitation…indecision…uncertainty…doubt…"

"I know what hesitation means, Mr Tanner."

"Samuel. Call me Samuel. Especially as we're going to be partners. You can't keep calling me Mr Tanner then, can you?"

"Partners? Did you say partners?"

"Yes."

And then he smiled right up to his forehead, the lines there in total agreement with his mouth and eyes. He oozed charm. He knew it. And would have pushed more out if he'd thought he needed to. His head tilted to the left as he watched her expression flitting from disbelief to outrage to amusement.

"All right, Samuel. Why don't you tell me in what enterprise you'd like me to be in partnership with you?"

It was Samuel's turn to be surprised. He had expected more of a battle.

"I'm taking over my parents' bookshop. It's called *The Bookcase*. Perhaps you know it?"

"Yes, I do," she said quietly, leaning forward, her forearms out flat on her desk. Heads were raised at nearby desks, curiosity in the eyes looking at them.

"Well, I'm an accountant, as you know," he stage-whispered, looking over his shoulder. "I can do the financial side. But I don't know much about books…"

"No," she said dryly.

He held up his arms in defeat. "I know. I know. That should tell you why I'd make a frightful mess of it if I tried to do it by myself, or with someone less qualified than yourself." He stopped for a moment. "You are qualified, I take it?"

"As a librarian, yes."

"Well, exactly!"

"And what makes you think I'd want to leave all this?" she asked, indicating her surroundings.

"Too stifling. You'll suffocate here," he said positively. "You need a challenge. Something to do for yourself."

"But this is my chosen career."

"Yes, but one you can branch out from. Spread your wings."

She regarded him without answering, her dark eyes betraying nothing of her feelings.

"Look," he said, "I need a decision now. If you don't come in with me, then I'll sell *The Bookcase*."

She stood and held out her hand to him. "I accept."

During his teens, Samuel had attended the many society balls that were an expected obligation, if not enjoyment, and his younger, slimmer figure was often seen expertly guiding a pretty debutante around a dance floor. The infinite number of fluttering hopeful hearts regarded Samuel Tanner as a 'good catch' and they made no secret of their interest. He was, however, rarely seen with the same girl twice and never made a practise of bringing any of them home to meet his parents. When he returned from Europe, his parents were hopeful that he would meet 'the right girl' but were disappointed to see that nothing eventuated. At times they would bring up the subject of grandchildren—a subject that would cause their son to become uncomfortable and he would skilfully divert the conversation to other things. By the time Frances came into Samuel's life, his parents were genuinely concerned that the grandchildren they so wanted would never materialize. Frances's appearance caused them to smile with relief and they waited eagerly for the announcement of an impending marriage. She would fit the bill of daughter-in-law and provider of grandchildren beautifully.

Helen Tanner stood at the front door of her home as Samuel stopped his car in front of the gate.

"How she knows when I'll be here is beyond me," Samuel laughed.

"Do you think she's been standing there for long?" Frances asked.

"Probably since I rang and confirmed the other day. Can't you see the cobwebs and dust all over her?"

"Samuel!"

He opened the car door for Frances and turned as his mother walked along the path to open the gate. He gave her a hug.

"You smell like roses," he observed.

"Your father's gift of perfume," she smiled.

"Nice." He kissed her on the neck.

"Get out with you, Samuel Tanner!"

Frances stood back watching them. Their closeness was touching to see. A quick pang of envy rushed through her. Helen was soft, cuddly, welcoming. Her short, permed grey hair was neatly arranged around a friendly face that was quick to smile. A lively, intelligent expression filled her eyes as she regarded the world around her with enthusiastic interest. At seventy-seven, the top of her head reached just under her son's chin, her own chin waggling loosely as her head moved from side to side whilst engaged in conversation.

"And Frances. At last!"

"Hello, Helen. It's good to see you. Thank you for inviting me—again." She handed Helen a bunch of tightly wrapped long-stemmed roses.

"Oh, Frances, you know you shouldn't," Helen gushed.

"But I want to," Frances insisted quietly.

"You know you're always welcome, dear—without the necessity of gifts." She kissed Frances and took her arm. "Come inside. Both of you. There are some hot scones waiting in the kitchen."

"I can smell them from here." Samuel's voice came from the open window of the car. He started up the engine. "I'll take the car around to the garage, Mother, and bring our luggage in through the back." He looked at Frances. "Don't you eat all those scones before I get there."

"Oh, get out with you," his mother laughed.

A row of small bottles was lined up in the centre of the kitchen table. Howard Tanner reached out for one of them and shook a capsule out of it.

"Blasted things," he grumbled. "I'll start to rattle soon."

"You haven't finished your scone," Helen observed.

"I'm not hungry."

"Still feeling nauseous, Dad?" Samuel looked concerned.

"Yes, Son."

"Your father eats hardly a thing I put in front of him these days. If I didn't know better, I'd say he didn't like my cooking!"

"Never did like it." Howard tried to look convincing but the others only laughed. A mischievous grin broke over his face, despite himself, and he winked at his son as he passed a hand over his head, making sure his sparse silver hair was in place over a bald patch.

"Oh, sure, Dad," Samuel chuckled, "that's why you weighed fourteen stone most of your life!"

"Don't weigh that now. Food's gone off."

"I see what you mean," Samuel tut-tutted. "Can I have another scone, Mother?"

"I thought the food was off," Helen retorted.

"Can't have them going to waste, can I?"

Frances joined in on the joke. "What a supreme sacrifice! I think I'd better join you."

"Another cup of tea, dear?" Helen offered her.

Frances held out her cup. Not for the first time, she marvelled at the easy-going, trusting and loving relationship that was shared by the Tanners. In her own experience, she had nothing to compare it with; she enjoyed their affectionate banter and the way Samuel was included in everything. They even included Frances.

Howard turned to Samuel, his wrinkled fingers habitually rolling and unrolling the edge of the table cloth in front of him. "How's the shop going, Son?"

"Oh, great, Dad, thanks to Frances."

"Don't be silly," Frances scolded, embarrassed. "It's your accountancy skills, the budgets you set, the lack of bad debts. You don't need me."

"Don't be so modest," he smiled. "Without your knowledge of the literary world, where would the shop be? Since I enticed you away from the library, the business has doubled."

"He's right," Howard nodded. "Even before I got this blasted disease the business was never as profitable as it is now. Helen and I—we didn't know anywhere near as much as you do about books."

Frances felt her face turning red. "What utter nonsense! It's always been a successful book shop."

"Yes," Helen joined in, "but now it's the most respected book shop in Melbourne. Look at the custom you've built up! Samuel's right, dear. We were so fortunate to find you." She leaned across the table to squeeze Frances's hand.

Frances returned the squeeze, placing her hands over Helen's. "I'm glad Samuel did! I needed the change. And I love *The Bookcase*!" She turned to Howard. "But, what about you, Mr Tanner?"

"Howard! Howard! How many times have I got to tell you my name is Howard!"

"But…"

"No buts. What a stubborn girl this is!"

"Hopeless," Samuel agreed.

"Howard," Frances conceded. "Happy now?"

"Humph!" Howard feigned displeasure. "Maybe."

"Mr…Howard…tell me—how are you feeling? Is the new medication lessening the pain?"

"Which new medication? They give me so many blasted pills, I get mixed up! None of them work anyway." He swept his hand over the row of bottles, sending them in all directions as they tangled with the tablecloth. The others caught them before they rolled off the table.

Frances felt a pang of regret for having brought up the subject. "Are you in pain now?"

"He's always in pain," Helen said.

"I'm so sorry," Frances said quietly.

"It's all right, girlie." Howard raised a shaking hand to pass one of the bottles to his wife. "Can't be helped."

Helen leaned towards her husband. "You're looking tired, dear. How about a lie down?"

"I suppose so," he said weakly, pushing on his chair. Samuel helped him to his feet and passed him a walking frame. He began to shuffle out of the room.

"And you look tired too, Frances," Helen observed. "Would you like a rest? I've got your room ready."

"Thanks. I could do with forty winks."

"Come on then, dear. I'll tuck you both in. What about you Samuel?"

"I'm fine. I'll take Dad up to bed, if you like. Then I'll take advantage of the quiet and catch up on a bit of paper work this afternoon."

Howard turned back slowly to raise an arm towards Frances. "See you later on. Be right as rain then."

She smiled at him until the two men walked slowly out of the kitchen. When they were out of earshot she said, "He's not getting any better is he?"

"No, dear. Worse, in fact."

"I'm sorry."

"You know, he used to move so quickly before…before this. For the big man that he was."

"I wish I'd known him then," Frances said wistfully, a hint of tears in her eyes.

Helen looked at her in concern. "But you're looking so pale, dear, and very dark around the eyes. Are you sickening for something?"

"Not really. I may have been overdoing things a bit…"

"Is that son of mine making you work too hard?"

"No. It's probably the move to my new place."

"Samuel should have been helping you—taking care of you."

"He does more than enough!" Frances protested.

Helen was adamant. "So he should." She hesitated. "How is the new place?"

"Oh, it's just what I was looking for."

"Have you got rowdy neighbours?"

"No, it's very peaceful," Frances assured her. "And it overlooks the gardens, just a stone's throw from *The Bookcase*."

"Samuel mentioned something about that. He said you hardly need your car."

"I might end up selling it. I never liked driving anyway. And it takes only minutes to walk to work." Frances stifled a yawn but Helen saw it.

"Here's me rattling on and you're tired!"

"I'm all right…"

"You rest dear. We'll catch up later."

Helen kissed Frances on the cheek and gently pushed her towards the stairway.

Samuel returned to the kitchen. "Dad's settled." He took up a tea towel and stood ready as Helen began to wash the few dishes.

"Oh, good," his mother smiled as she handed him a plate. "Frances looks very tired, Samuel. Is she doing too much?"

"I don't think so, Mother."

"You're looking after her?"

"As much as she'll let me," he laughed. "She's a very independent woman, you know."

"Yes, I know. Too independent for my liking!" She banged a saucer down for emphasis.

"There's not much we can do about that," he said, shaking the suds from the saucer.

"Yes there is."

"What?"

"*You* could change that." She looked hard at him, steam from the hot dish water fogging her glasses.

"How?"

"Oh, don't be so thick!" she snapped.

"What *are* you talking about, Mother?" Samuel stopped drying as he regarded his mother with surprise.

"Isn't it about time you and Frances got married?"

"Married?"

"Yes, married." Her voice softened. "You know how happy it'd make your father."

"Yes, but…"

"Especially now," she said, turning her attention to the sink so that he wouldn't see the tears that suddenly sprang to her eyes. "Before it's too late…"

"Mother, you know I love Frances." He put down his tea towel and turned her by the shoulders so that he could look her in the eye.

"So…why haven't you asked her?" she sniffed.

He laughed ruefully, "She'd probably say no."

"Ask her, dear. Then you can both settle down."

"We are settled!"

"Yes—separately! You shouldn't have let her buy that new apartment."

"How could I stop her?"

"Ridiculous! You living in one place, and her in another." Helen resumed her washing at a furious pace.

"I can't tell her what to do," he replied helplessly.

"You're almost too old to have children—and I did *so* want to be a grandmother." She looked at him with hope. "But it's not too late."

"My God! Do you know what you're asking?"

"Yes. Your father and I…we want some grandchildren before we die. It's not much to ask, you know."

'It's too late for me…"

"Not for Frances," she insisted.

"She doesn't want marriage—or children."

"How do you know? Have you asked her?"

"Not directly. No. But I know her. I should after all this time."

"Every woman wants children!"

"Not *every* woman. Not Frances."

"What would *you* know about women?" she snapped.

Samuel looked at her in dismay, searching her face for any clue as to what she meant by the remark. He rummaged his mind in a confused state for something to say.

His mother continued. "I mean, we never see you with anyone other than Frances. What gives you the right to comment on women's childbearing wants and needs. How could you possibly know?"

"Don't get me wrong, Mother." He held up his hands in surrender. "I was only saying…"

"Please, Samuel. It would make us very happy to see you and Frances marry. It would make you happy too."

She kissed him soundly on the cheek and smiled to herself as she turned back to the sink.

Frances woke as afternoon sunlight splashed across her face through a chink in the curtains. She stretched luxuriously, snuggling deeper into the warmth of the blankets, surprised that she'd slept for nearly three hours. Her eyes meandered lazily around the bedroom. It was a welcoming room that she always felt at home in. The double bed was adorned with a ruffled bedspread that matched the draped curtains and pillows piled high for resting against when reading. The bedside tables had pretty antique glass lamps vying for position amongst a clutter of framed photographs of Samuel at various stages of his life, an antique clock, and a drinking glass and matching water jug with a beaded lace cover draped over it. In the drawers were tissues, paper, envelopes, pens, postage stamps and little jars of herbal hand creams. On the wall facing the bed, and beside a cushioned armchair, was a bookcase completely full of books that satisfied all tastes. A vase of freshly-picked flowers sat on top of the bookcase, giving the room a final welcoming touch.

Frances imagined Helen pottering around the garden looking for just the right flowers to pick for her guest. She knew that the older woman would have derived much pleasure from the simple task and that she would have shown the vase to Howard who would have complemented her upon the artistic arrangement.

The peace of the country town contrasted profoundly with the clatter of trams and chaos of city traffic that were part of Frances's everyday life. Here the absence of noise was strange—almost deafening—in the way her ears strained to hear the slightest sound carried on the breeze. A bird broke into song outside her window, a dog barked somewhere far off, a child's voice mingled with that of another in conversation that trickled past the house along with muffled footsteps on the grassed sidewalk.

A door banged shut somewhere downstairs and Helen's tinkling laughter floated up to Frances's ears. *Okay lazy bones, get up and join them,* she scolded herself as she threw the covers back and jumped out of bed. In a matter of minutes she'd washed her face, pulled on a jumper and slacks and was downstairs peeling potatoes and carrots for the evening's roast dinner.

This was a precious time for Frances. She felt comfortable with the Tanners who, since she'd known them, gave her a feeling of belonging in a family environment. But a part of her held back just enough to protect herself from possible rejection. It was difficult for her to believe that they could accept her wholeheartedly. Many times she asked herself what she could possibly offer them in return. She felt guilty accepting their hospitality suspecting that they saw something more than mere friendship in her relationship with Samuel. At times Frances pictured herself in the role of Mrs Samuel Tanner, the wife and daughter-in-law who would legitimately visit and therefore not be taking advantage of their kindness. But the picture always faded into nothingness. She knew Samuel would only ever be a friend—never a lover. And so she looked at Helen's kindly face, full of expectation as she prattled on about the next time Frances would visit and that she hoped it would be longer than just a weekend and not so long between visits, and Frances felt guilty all over again.

Dinner was a noisy affair with lively conversation bandied around the dining room table. After two bottles of wine and plates piled high with roast lamb and vegetables, Frances helped Helen to clear the table for a game of Scrabble. The room was warm with a roaring open fire casting a cheerful glow onto the proceedings. Howard made great ceremony of opening a bottle of thirty year-old port and they settled down to the game with a Mozart symphony playing softly in the background. None of them spoke for several minutes as they concentrated on the letters they had in front of them. It was Helen's turn; she quickly added a word to the board using two blank tiles. She looked from Samuel to Frances in triumph.

"There!" She sat back in her seat looking smug.

"What is it?" Howard asked, peering at the tiles as he adjusted his glasses.

"Marriage, of course," she replied. "What a *nice* word!"

An embarrassed silence followed with both Frances and Samuel looking intently at their tiles. Howard, seemingly unaware of the sudden tension in the air, held out the port bottle towards Helen's empty glass but she ignored him.

"Don't you think so, Samuel?" she said beaming at her son.

Samuel cleared his throat. "Yes, Mother. Very clever. You've used all your tiles too."

"Don't you think so, Frances?" Helen asked, turning to pat Frances's hand.

"Yes, Helen. You got a big score with that one."

"No," Helen insisted. "I mean the actual word. I'm surprised you haven't thought of it yourself."

"Mother…" Samuel frowned.

Howard started laughing, which resulted in a coughing fit lasting several minutes. Samuel tapped his father on the back until the fit subsided. "You know your mother, Son. She won't give up." He handed the port bottle to Samuel who topped up everyone's glasses.

Frances busied herself with shuffling her Scrabble tiles around on the wooden stand. Despite her hair falling over her face as she bent forward, her flushed cheeks betrayed her embarrassment.

Frances rose early the next morning, dressed quietly and let herself out of the house without waking anyone. The morning was crisp but sunny, and she enjoyed a brisk walk to Daylesford Lake where she walked along a path that led around the water's edge. She paused for a moment on a small bridge that was on the opposite side of the lake to The Boathouse restaurant. The last time she and Samuel had visited his parents had been in the summer and they had sat out on the deck and enjoyed a meal whilst being observed by the ducks and other wild birds that frequented the lake. Now all was deserted by human presence, but the chorus of bird calls was overwhelming as the business of finding breakfast for demanding feathered youngsters took precedence. Frances smiled to herself as a mynah returned to its nest where a collection of tiny beaks protruded skywards, open and expectant. She watched as the parent fed its young, until a plop in the water nearby distracted her. A school of fish glided underneath the bridge and disappeared under the reflecting water's surface near the shore.

When she returned to the house, the smell of frying bacon greeted Frances's nostrils and hunger stimulated her mouth to watering.

"I don't know how I could possibly be hungry after last night's huge dinner," she laughed as she entered the kitchen.

"Of course you are, dear," Helen smiled in return. "It's the good country air does it."

Despite herself, Frances made a good meal of the huge breakfast Helen dished up for them, although she noticed that Howard only picked at his food. She refrained from commenting as she noticed the concerned expression in Helen's eyes. Samuel looked at Frances and shook his head slightly as if to say, *there's nothing we can do about it.* The row of pill bottles lined up in front of Howard said it all as far as Frances was concerned.

The rest of the day passed by pleasantly enough with a visit to the local galleries and Frances being tempted to buy a Richard Weatherly print. She found herself being drawn back to it time and again until Samuel finally said, "Well, are you going to buy it or not?"

"I'll be sorry if I don't," she admitted.

"Well, if you don't, I will," he grinned. "I like it too."

"I'll fight you for it," she laughed, and held up her hand to the saleswoman.

Back at the Tanner's home she held up the print to show Samuel's parents.

"It's called *Mountain Ash and Crimson Rosellas,*" she explained, as they admired the intricately-drawn print showing three rosellas flying amongst a forest landscape of trees with peeling bark. "It'll be perfect in my lounge room."

"We almost came to fisticuffs over it," Samuel laughed. "She threatened to boil me in oil if I bought it for my place."

"I can just see her doing that," Howard guffawed. "Right little spitfire, eh?"

Helen said quietly to herself but loud enough to be heard by the others, "If you were living in the same place there wouldn't be a problem, would there?"

Howard chuckled at his wife's temerity while Frances and Samuel suddenly busied themselves repacking the print and getting ready to leave.

At the front gate, Howard leaned heavily on his walking frame, exhausted by the effort of walking from the house but triumphant that he'd achieved his goal. They waved as Samuel's car turned towards Melbourne.

"Don't leave it so long next time," Helen called out to Frances. "We love having you stay."

They sat back in the car without speaking for some moments until Samuel broke the silence. "She lays it on a bit thick sometimes."

Frances smiled.

"You know what mothers are like," he added.

There was a pause. "No. I don't."

Chapter 6

The poignant despair of the final movement of Tchaikovsky's *Pathétique* affected the whole audience sitting mesmerized by the emotional expression of personal suffering in the composer's life. As the violins and cellos responded to each other in the sombre mood, Frances wept silently, unconsciously. So immersed was she in the beauty and melancholy of the music, that she was no longer aware of herself or her surroundings. She was transported to another place, another time.

The concertmaster's broad shoulders moved fluidly under the black fabric of his tuxedo as he guided the bow across the strings of his violin. He sat on the edge of his seat, balancing his weight on the ball of his right foot as a great cat might before it pounces. He played with the ease and confidence of an accomplished musician, the violin an extension of himself.

At forty years of age, Adam Harcourt was a tall, solid man who was uncomfortable at times with his inner sensibilities which seemed at odds with his masculine outer shell. He was a likeable handsome man, one who naturally attracted the attentions of the opposite sex, and at the same time a man who was genuinely admired by other men who sought his friendship. An instinctive leader, patient teacher, and gifted musician, Adam was a good shoulder to lean on in either a professional or personal capacity. Quick to sense another's distress, he was always ready to listen and share a problem, offer advice, and help if he could. His hazel eyes held an intelligent compassion as they regarded someone else. When in a serious or thoughtful attitude, his subject would be the sole focus of those eyes. They were hooded by slightly arched eyebrows matching exactly his light brown hair. Pronounced single lines swept down from the rounded curves of his nostrils to below the corners of his mouth.

It was a sensitive full mouth, the corners of which would quiver slightly before smiling—and that was often. His jaw was square, firm, strong, cleft with a shallow dimple.

As he played, his eyes strayed from the conductor to sweep across the audience in front of him. This particular symphony had always moved him, and this time was no exception. He imagined he could feel the great composer's pain, his torment, his sense of approaching death and, as the last notes died away in a hushed whisper, his gaze stopped again at Frances. He had noticed earlier her emotional reaction to music and was both surprised and pleased by it. *This is a sensitive soul,* he thought. The tears, caught in the reflection of the stage lights, glistened on her cheeks as her head moved slightly. But she made no effort to dry them. She appeared as if in a trance.

After a momentary hesitance on the part of the audience, when it took a collective sigh of satisfied sadness, an outpouring of gratitude for the orchestra's interpretation of Tchaikovsky's music was realised in heartfelt applause. The conductor's mop of thick black hair flipped forward over his bowed head and then flew back as he straightened and took the applause. He indicated different sections of the orchestra as they stood to receive their share of audience approval. Adam noticed a flicker of white lace that Frances surreptitiously dabbed at her wet face. The handkerchief was gone as quickly as it had appeared. The conductor held out his hand and Adam shook it before resuming his seat along with the rest of the orchestra. The clapping died down gradually after the conductor had walked offstage and reappeared four more times. Adam watched Frances incline her head to a man seated beside her. He wondered if the man was her husband. The string section took its final bow before vacating the stage. Adam turned to see Frances leaving her seat with her arm through that of the man who had been speaking to her. She was smiling at something her companion was saying, but her face still held a haunted expression. *It's like looking at two people on the one face,* he thought, *but one face is lying.*

Frances poured boiling water into the coffee plunger and placed it on a tray which she carried into the loungeroom where Samuel was seated in an armchair looking through the concert programme.

He pushed his spectacles down to the end of his nose and looked over them at her. "Do you ever get lonely here, all by yourself?" he asked as she put the tray on a coffee table in front of him.

"Why, Samuel," she laughed. "I've never been lonely. I like living alone. You know that."

"Yes, I know."

An eyebrow shot up in surprise. "Why then?"

"Oh," he shrugged. "I just wondered." He took his spectacles off and folded them carefully into a silver case.

Frances looked at him thoughtfully then sat down to pour the coffee. "Have you spoken with your mother since the weekend?"

"Yes. I rang her before picking you up tonight. I forgot to tell you."

"How's your father?"

"No worse," Samuel said, accepting a cup. "Mother's terribly worried though."

"She can't cope on her own much longer, can she?"

"I don't think so."

"What then? A nursing home?"

"Probably. Though she doesn't want to put him in one until she has to."

"She's a brave woman."

"Yes, she is." Samuel took a sip of his coffee then looked at Frances over the rim of his cup. "You know, she spoke to me about you."

"Oh?"

He watched her carefully as he continued. "You know they want us to marry."

"What...?" Frances's own cup rattled in its saucer.

"They think the world of you. And they want grandchildren."

"My God!" She put down her cup and saucer, looking aghast at him.

"Would you marry me...if I asked you?"

"Samuel, you know that..."

"Would you?" he insisted.

"I...I couldn't," she floundered. "It wouldn't be fair."

"To whom?"

"To you. To me."

"Why?"

"I don't think you want to marry me," she said slowly, "or anyone."

"Mother says..."

"No. It's not what your mother wants. It's you. You don't need or want me."

There was a long pause as they regarded each other. Frances struggled with herself, biting her lip, wondering if she should say any more.

"I don't believe you want any woman," she said finally, quietly.

"What do you mean by that?"

"You know what I mean."

"Do I?"

She saw a pulse jumping in his neck.

"Yes," she said slowly. "You do."

Frances felt as if her heart had stopped as they stared at each other. The background music from her stereo, and Plato's purring as she stroked him absent-mindedly, were the only sounds in the room. Warily, she decided to go ahead.

"I know that you're homosexual," she said plainly, though she needed to clear her throat after she'd said it. "I've known for a long time."

Samuel rose from his chair and stood for several moments looking out of the window, his back to her. She wondered if he was breathing as he seemed as if turned to stone. Perhaps, she thought, his blood had frozen, or his muscles were unable to move, or his mind had seized with hatred for her. She watched him, waiting for something—anything. At last he straightened his shoulders and adjusted his tie, his head moving from side to side, then turned to face her.

His face was stiff. "They don't know."

"I know that."

"It would kill them."

"Would it?"

"Yes."

"Don't you think they would accept you as you are?"

"Never! You know my father. I'm the only child…you know, to carry on the line. And especially now. It would finish him off. Why do you think I've hidden it all these years?"

"Is that why you associate with me," she asked thoughtfully, "…as a cover?"

He sat beside her on the couch and took her hands in his.

"No." His voice was earnest. "I love you."

"Like a…sister?"

"Well…yes. I suppose so."

"That's all right. But you wouldn't ask a sister to marry you."

"No, I wouldn't," he agreed.

"And what about you? Your happiness. Isn't it difficult for you…?"

The corners of his mouth pulled downwards. "You get used to it."

"The world has changed, Samuel." She reached up to touch his face. "It's not so condemnatory—like it used to be. Surely you could be more open about it? At least here—away from your parents?"

He shook his head. "I'm not prepared to risk it. Not while they're still alive."

"And your…friends…friend? Do they…does he…want that?"

"My…friend…he would like acknowledgment…of our relationship. He even wants to meet you. Has done for years. But I can't…won't."

"Is that fair? To either of you?"

"It can't be helped. It's just the way it is," Samuel shrugged, "…has been, for a long time."

"I'm sorry."

"So am I."

"Look—nothing's changed. We're still the same." She laughed weakly. "Just don't ask me to marry you again." Then she stopped as something occurred to her. "But why did you ask me?"

"I thought—well, you're not getting any younger."

"Oh, come on! Spare me the heroics. Surely you wouldn't have gone through with it?"

"For you I would."

"What about you? Your friend? Wouldn't he feel betrayed?"

"He'd understand."

"Understand! How could your lover understand your marrying me? Don't you care about his feelings?"

"He knows about you. You'd be no threat to him."

"How would *you* feel if he married a woman?" she retorted.

"That's not the issue."

"Oh no? And when would you meet him if I was around all the time? Would we make it a cosy threesome?"

He looked shocked. "Don't be vulgar!"

She tossed her hair back off her face. "I'd like to meet him."

"Why?"

"Because he's…part of you, I guess."

"So you can have a look at the freakish side of me?" Samuel's mouth had become a thin, hard line. His eyes changed from pale blue to icy grey.

"It's not like that."

"I know." He was suddenly contrite. "Sorry."

"Well, why not?"

"It would complicate things too much."

"I would have thought it would make things easier for you. Get it out in the open. At least with me? I'm in no position to judge and wouldn't want to anyway."

"I'd rather not right now." He frowned. "Things have been a little...rocky...lately."

Understanding dawned upon her. "You haven't told him you were going to ask me to marry you?"

"Yes, I did."

"My God! How could you! It must have hurt him terribly."

"He said he understood."

Frances threw her hands in the air. "I can't believe what you're suggesting! And what about your parents? It would have been a farce! Do you need me as a smokescreen that badly?"

"To be quite honest, yes," he said simply, "but it would have been a *hands-off* arrangement that suited us both."

"What do you mean...both?"

"Just that." He looked at her closely. "You're using me as much as I'm using you."

"Using you? How can you say that?"

"Well, aren't you? There's nothing intimate in our relationship. And I've never seen you with other men. So, what's your excuse?"

"I just..."

"I don't think you're a lesbian?"

"No, I'm not!"

"Well," he said deliberately, "why is a beautiful woman like you going out with a man like me?"

There was ice in her eyes. "I don't wish to discuss the matter." She stood, looking down at him where he remained seated on the couch. "I'm tired."

He got to his feet, knowing instinctively that any further argument would be useless. "As you wish," he said quietly, "but one day we'll talk about you."

Samuel walked stiffly out of the room and let himself out without looking back. The door closed behind him with a soft click. She stared at the closed door for some minutes, her eyes glazed, until Plato rubbed up against her legs. Startled out of her trance, she bent to pick him up. He began to purr as she stroked him distractedly.

Then she burst into tears.

Chapter 7

Adam looked through the glass pane in the door that led onto the stage. Most of the other members of the orchestra were already there warming their instruments and waiting for his appearance. The principal cello joined him.

"Full house again tonight," he commented to Adam as he made his way past.

"They love the fifth," Adam said.

"Who doesn't?"

The muted sound of many voices was clearly discernible from where Adam stood. He felt the exciting rush of adrenaline that always preceded a performance; this was where he belonged.

An oboist rushed past him, patting her hair into place.

"Bloody traffic," she mumbled to herself. "Why can't they…" And the rest of the sentence was lost as the door swung to.

Adam saw that the full complement of the orchestra was ready as he peeped through the glass again, and he entered the stage to the applause of the audience. As he made his way to the front of the stage, he noticed Frances and Samuel seated in the front row. He smiled inwardly, and had just enough time to admit to himself that he'd been watching out for her at every performance, before turning towards the orchestra. He indicated to the oboist to give the 'A'.

The solo trumpet fanfare opened the Mahler *Fifth Symphony* taking the audience on an emotional journey to the fourth movement —the *Adagietto*. The notes from Adam's violin fused and separated from the other strings as he played, eyes mostly closed, lost in the beauty of the slow movement. His passion soared with the familiar ache in his throat. His ears tingled with the cacophony of sound that enveloped him. His rhythmic bowing lulled him.

With the mood broken by the french horn in the final movement, Adam's eyes opened to focus upon the conductor and then swept around to the front row of the audience. His eyes locked upon those of Frances who had been watching him intently. Startled, she looked away, scanning the rest of the orchestra, deliberately stopping at each section, yet aware of Adam's gaze. He played on, willing her to look back at him. Irresistibly, her eyes were drawn back and, seeing him watching her, she flushed. She looked down at her lap in embarrassment, twisting a lace handkerchief between her fingers. Samuel sensed her movement beside him and turned with an eyebrow raised, his forehead a collection of lines. He touched her lightly on the hand. The twisting stopped and she smiled at his look of query. Satisfied, Samuel's attention returned to the stage. Tears blurred her vision as the music recaptured her and she lived inside Mahler's emotions until the final tumultuous bars of the symphony were met with rapturous applause.

A large woman and her equally large partner jostled Frances as she waited for Samuel during interval. Frances could just see the top of Samuel's head amongst the crowd of people waiting to be served at the bar. She looked down again at her programme, making use of the time to familiarize herself with the background of the Brahms piano concerto to be performed next. Engrossed in her reading, she failed to notice Adam making his way slowly through the crowd, searching each face, moving towards her. He stopped when he recognised her as she raised her head to check on Samuel's progress. Returning to her programme, she read a few lines until she became aware of someone standing in front of her. Without looking up, she took in the polished black shoes, the black trousers, a faint whiff of aftershave.

"May I join you?" The unfamiliar voice played teasingly around her ears.

"Why…yes," she replied as she looked up, startled, aware of a spreading blush that reached her cheeks.

"Are you enjoying the performance this evening?"

The hazel eyes smiled along with the upturned corners of his mouth that quivered slightly.

"Very much," she said, a little uncertainly, as she recognised him. "Why, you're…"

"Frances?" Samuel interrupted, surprised to find her in conversation with a stranger. He handed her a glass of champagne, and turned to her companion with interest.

"Samuel, dear," she smiled as she took the glass. "I was just talking to Mr … I'm sorry?"

"Harcourt. Adam Harcourt."

Adam held out his hand to Samuel. They shook hands.

"Samuel Tanner," he declared, still puzzled.

Adam turned to Frances, his eyes holding a faintly amused expression. "And you are…?"

"I'm sorry," Samuel said, putting his hand on Frances's arm. "This is Frances Draper."

Frances offered her hand to Adam.

"I'm very pleased to know you," he said, taking her hand. The fact that Frances and Samuel had different surnames had not escaped him.

She noticed the warmth of his palm and long fingers as they covered her own for a moment.

"Yes, I…"

He had a dimple in his firm, square jaw, she saw. And the corners of his mouth were still quivering. She wondered if he was trying not to laugh.

"Can I get you a drink, Mr Harcourt?" Samuel offered.

"Adam…please."

"Adam, then."

"No, thank you. Not while I'm working."

"Oh?" Samuel paused, then recognition dawned upon him as he took in Adam's clothes. "Then you're a member of the orchestra?"

"Yes."

"You're the concertmaster." Frances was quite sure now.

"Oh, of course. Excuse me," Samuel said, embarrassed. "I should have realised."

"Not at all," Adam smiled. "There are a lot of people on the stage."

"Do you mingle with the audience as a rule, Adam?" Samuel looked at him closely.

"No, not really."

Adam looked at Frances's left hand as it clutched the champagne flute. He noticed that she was wearing no rings; in fact she wore very little jewellery at all. She appeared nervous; a vein pulsated in her neck, a faint flicker underneath the skin.

They were interrupted by the bells ringing to announce the return of the audience to their seats.

"I have to go," Adam said quickly.

Frances glanced at his eyes, his nose, his mouth, as he spoke. She hoped he couldn't hear the sound of her heart beating as it roared in her ears.

"Enjoy the concerto," he said over his shoulder.

"Yes…" her voice came out a croak as he disappeared into the crowd.

Samuel looked at her closely. He frowned as she looked around for a place to put her empty glass but, with unusual clumsiness, only just succeeded in not dropping it. He refrained from comment as they made their way to their seats. They sat in an uncomfortable silence as the audience settled and the orchestra prepared for the next item.

Fugue

When Adam was satisfied the orchestra was tuned, he sat to wait for the conductor and the guest pianist. He saw that Frances and Samuel were seated and he smiled openly at them. Samuel nodded in gruff acknowledgement. Frances smiled tentatively and then looked down at her hands. She was glad they were in her lap where they couldn't betray their shaking in the dim light.

The pianist lifted his coat tails as he sat on the piano stool. He took his cue from the conductor and raised his hands to the keyboard. They hovered, waiting, the spotlight catching the hairs on the backs of his fingers. A french horn preceded the pianist's first chords and then the familiar concerto transported Frances to another time.

> The hands on the keyboard are white. The long smooth fingers taper to perfect nails painted blood-red. The black open-toed shoe provides a glimpse of the same polish on the toenails as the foot moves on the pedal. Frances sees her mother's diamond ring sparkle under the lights as she moves her hands across the keyboard. From her front row seat, Frances sees her father seated with the orchestra. His eyes never leave his wife's back as his bow sweeps across the strings of his violin. Frances wills her parents to look at her, acknowledge her. If she reaches out, she can almost touch them. Her hand extends to the stage edge, the tips of her fingers just connecting with the blonde wood. Her mother bends over the keyboard, her hands darting across it in a frantic blur. Her father's features are frozen in concentration. Neither is aware of their daughter. Imperceptibly at first, the stage begins to recede, then gradually the space between the front row and her parents increases until it races away from her. They are mere dots in the distance when she screams soundlessly for them. She knows she must not make a sound in the concert hall. It is forbidden.

Behind Frances a man coughed, bringing her back to the present. She blinked rapidly as her vision cleared. Droplets of perspiration flew from the pianist's forehead as his hands coaxed the last notes of the concerto from the keys. As one, the piano and the orchestra ceased to exist in the immediate silence commanded by the conductor. Then applause broke the spell and a look of satisfied relief spread across the features of the aging pianist as he bowed.

As Samuel joined the standing ovation, Adam watched, fascinated, while Frances quickly dabbed at her eyes and cheeks with the lace handkerchief. He saw her blink an expression of utter melancholy from her face, to be replaced by one of composure, aloofness—almost frigidity—as it seeped through the pores until it covered her face. She rose to stand beside Samuel, clapping enthusiastically as the pianist returned to the stage. Her eyes strayed to Adam and her hands froze momentarily when she realised he had been watching her.

Frances hid a discreet yawn behind her hand as Samuel drew his car to a halt outside her apartment building.

"… funny about that violinist turning up like that, though."

"Who…Adam?" she replied as she opened her handbag.

"Yes, that Harcourt chap."

"Well, it's nice to meet members of the orchestra."

"Member." Samuel turned to look at her, taking his hands from the wheel. "Singular."

"Yes," Frances said noncommittally. She found her keys and snapped her handbag shut.

"I wonder what he was doing mixing with the public?"

"It's probably good PR for the orchestra."

"Is that what you call it?"

"Pardon?" She looked at Samuel, startled, aware of the sarcasm in his voice.

"I don't think it was PR. I think it was you."

"Whatever do you mean?"

"You. I think he wanted to meet you."

"What on earth for?"

"I think he's attracted to you."

"How could he be? He doesn't even know me!"

"I think he'd like to know you."

Frances pulled the door lock up. "Don't be silly."

"No…really. The way he was looking at you."

"How ridiculous!" She opened the door.

"He kept on looking at you during the performance too. I saw him."

"He wouldn't be able to see that far."

"If we can see him, he can see us."

"It's too dark."

"Not in the front row of the stalls where we are."

"Your imagination's running away with you tonight," she frowned.

"I don't think so," he insisted.

"Well, I'm tired," she said, swinging her legs out onto the footpath. "I'm going up to bed."

Samuel made as if to get out of the car. "I'll just open the…"

"Don't worry. I've got it."

"Oh, all right. Goodnight, Dear."

"Goodnight."

She leaned back to offer her cheek to him. He kissed her lightly and she got out of the car.

"Sweet dreams," he called out, but the door closed upon his words.

He watched her walk up to the entrance and climb the short flight of steps. She turned to wave to him as she unlocked the door. He started up the engine and pulled the car smoothly out onto the road.

Fugue

A car whisked along Albert Street, its headlights casting a quick splash of light through the open curtains up and over the ceiling of Frances's bedroom. Her eyes blinked at the invasion of the dim light in which she'd been staring at the overhead light fitting. She had been trying to push something out of her mind so that she could go to sleep but she wasn't succeeding. The image was that of the new concertmaster. His dimpled chin, amused eyes and smiling mouth fluttered across the ceiling in separate fragments. She fancied she could even hear his voice and sense his aftershave. *Ridiculous!* She turned over on her side and was startled to see two luminous eyes staring at her.

"Oh, all right," she said.

Plato jumped up on the bed and settled down quickly around Frances's feet.

"I shouldn't let you get used to it, you know," Frances yawned. "Don't you move now, or you'll keep me awake."

She closed her eyes and drifted off to the rhythmic sound of Plato's purring.

Frances sits in the front row of an empty auditorium. Her legs swing from the edge of the seat, not touching the floor. The stage is crammed with a full orchestra. Frances's mother is seated at the piano and her father is playing the violin from his position of concertmaster. Although every member of the orchestra is playing, the only sound is that of applause. Eleanor turns her head towards her daughter as her hands fly across the keyboard. She appears as annoyed as her husband, Robert, who is also staring at Frances. The applause swells to a roar. Robert mouths, *Go away* to Frances. His voice gradually becomes a distinct echo; the words *Go away* repeat over and over as the applause becomes softer. Eleanor joins in and the two voices echo louder and louder. Frances stands and turns around to walk out. The concert hall seats are now at least three times her height and extend empty to the horizon. She begins to walk with difficulty in bogging sand, the words

66

Go away echoing in bass voices with each step she takes. She turns back to the stage but her parents wave her away. Frances reaches her hands out to them, tears pouring down her face, and she screams, *Mummy! Daddy!* but the voices continue echoing *Go away*. Frances begins to sink in the sand and the stage recedes until the orchestra is on the other horizon. She is sinking up to her neck and screams again for her parents. Her mouth fills with sand.

Frances woke with a start, drenched in perspiration, her cover twisted around her and a pillow over her face. Plato was sitting beside her head, watching her intently.

"What are you doing up here," she scolded.

A low rumble of pleasure greeted her words.

She patted him. "You were worried about me, eh?" She pushed him back to the foot of the bed. "Go on. Back down there."

They both settled down again in the dark and before long Frances sensed that Plato was sleeping. The images of Adam were now replaced with those of her parents as she remembered the nightmare. An old familiar ache in her throat had her blinking back tears with memories of her unhappy childhood. *No, she shouted in her mind, I will not let you hurt me anymore.* And she stared at the dim shape of the light fitting, counting from one thousand backwards in twos, concentrating solely on the numbers, until sleep claimed her again.

The steam from Frances's coffee mug drifted between her eyes and her view of the gardens on the other side of the road. She frowned as she looked back down at a review she had been trying to read. *Yet for all her poetic passion for her work, she is keenly aware that...* The gardens claimed her attention again while she took a sip of her coffee. She sighed and looked again at the sentence where her index finger marked the spot. *Yet for all her poetic...* She read it again. *Yet for all her poetic...*

Samuel handed his customer $1.50 change, along with two books, and watched as the customer left the shop. He turned to Frances who looked pale and tired. He noticed the dark circles underneath her eyes.

"You don't look the best, dear."

"Don't I?" Her finger still pointed to the same sentence on the page.

"No, you don't."

Her eyes were drawn back to the gardens as she failed to comment. Samuel walked around to stand in front of her, breaking her view with his body. She blinked in surprise.

"Anything I can do?" he asked.

"No thanks."

"You want to talk about it?"

She shrugged. "I'm just not sleeping very well lately."

"Why? Is there something worrying you?"

"No. No. It's nothing." She tossed her hair back from her face. "I'll be fine."

"If you're not sleeping well, perhaps you should see your doctor?" Concern clouded Samuel's eyes.

"No. I'm fine." She drained her mug and walked over to the counter. "Now, I'll just ring Greg Watson and tell him his book has arrived."

Samuel felt slightly miffed at her refusal to confide in him. She'd seemed angry with him the night before when he'd brought up the subject of the concertmaster's obvious interest in her. *Quite defensive about it, too.* He watched her as she spoke on the phone and wondered if he was the cause of her lack of sleep—or perhaps the concertmaster was. She finished her conversation and turned to find him staring at her. Her face broke into a brilliant smile and he smiled back. *Imagining it,* he told himself with a shrug.

Chapter 8

Some weeks later, Frances and Samuel attended Hamer Hall again. During interval they stood, as usual, sipping their champagne and discussing the performance they'd just seen. Frances appeared unnerved, constantly looking over her shoulder and failing to meet Samuel's eye as he spoke.

"You seem distracted," he observed.

"Do I?"

"Expecting someone?"

"No."

"Feeling okay?"

"Umm…"

She stiffened suddenly as Adam appeared behind Samuel.

"What?" He followed her eyes and turned to see Adam.

"Hello," Adam said smoothly. "Nice to see you again."

Frances noticed the corners of his mouth quivering. "Yes," she whispered.

The two men shook hands.

"So, you're out fraternizing again, eh?" Samuel commented.

"Something like that." The lines at the side of Adam's face deepened into a smile.

Frances felt her heart thudding wildly and scolded herself inwardly for reacting to his presence. *What's wrong with me?* She avoided eye contact with him, finding herself suddenly lost for words, and allowed the two men to talk without her. She felt awkward without understanding why. Her eyes focused on Samuel's bright yellow silk tie as she fiddled with her string of pearls, and at the same time being acutely aware of how tall Adam was. Her head only just reached his shoulders. *Think of something to say! Don't stand here like an idiot…*

"…young Christy Sable played it when she won the ABC competition a few years back." Samuel's voice broke in upon her thoughts. He looked at Frances strangely.

"Yes, she was very good. She's got a brilliant future in front of her," Adam said.

"How long have you been playing the violin?" Samuel asked.

"Ever since I was a kid."

Say something!

Samuel continued. "So your parents are musicians too?"

"No. Not at all. Dad's a cabinet maker and Mum's a teacher."

"But they encouraged you?" Frances was surprised to hear her own voice.

"Not really." Adam smiled at her. "Dad and my brothers never understood my love for music. I got it from Mum. She'd play classical music when they weren't around. They hated it, actually."

"Did your father mind you becoming a musician?" she asked, relieved that her brain was working again.

"Yes, he did. He wanted me to take over the family business. Become a carpenter, like my brothers. I was the eldest, you see."

"You must have loved music a lot to risk his disapproval."

Adam's eyes held hers. "Passionately."

"Why the violin?" Samuel's voice seemed harsh after a momentary silence.

"As a choice of instrument?"

"Yes."

"I used to read to an elderly blind lady in our street and she gave me her old violin when she knew I loved classical music. She was quite a violinist herself."

"Did she teach you?" Frances asked.

"Yes, she did. It was quite honestly the blind leading the blind though," he grimaced. "I wasn't a very apt pupil."

"Well, you've certainly made up for it now." Frances blushed, fearing the sincere compliment might have sounded forced or clichéd.

"I've been fortunate," he replied modestly.

"And now?" Samuel interjected. "Is there a Mrs Harcourt?"

Frances held her breath as she noticed Adam's lips tighten. The softness left his eyes.

"Not anymore."

"Oh?" Samuel's eyebrows rose in question.

"I'm divorced," Adam said quietly.

Frances let her breath go slowly.

"I'm sorry," Samuel replied, uncomfortable.

"No need," Adam smiled. After a moment's silence he added, "She hated music, you know."

"Oh—how awful for you!" Frances looked shocked.

Adam's lips relaxed into a smile as he regarded her. "It was a bit rough for a while—but not anymore."

"I didn't mean to pry," Samuel apologised.

"No. No. No offense. What about you two? How long have you been married?"

"Married!" Frances was stunned.

"Our special kind of relationship doesn't need the bonds of marriage," Samuel said pompously. "Frances and I share a very close devotion to each other—both professionally and emotionally." He linked his arm through hers as her eyebrows shot up in surprise.

"Oh, I see," Adam said quietly.

"We've been together for years, you know."

Frances withdrew her arm. "Samuel…?"

"She's a fine woman." His look to Adam was triumphant.

"Samuel!"

They all looked up as the bell sounded for the end of interval.

"That's my call," Adam said.

"Goodbye." Frances held out her hand to him before she thought about it.

"Until next time," he replied, taking her hand inside his two large ones.

The skin on her hand tingled after he let go. She and Samuel watched in silence as his figure dissolved into the packed foyer. Samuel took her empty glass from her.

"Just what did you mean by all that?" she said, turning to him.

"What?"

"All that *close devotion* and *not needing the bonds of marriage* claptrap."

"Just letting him know how things are."

"And just how are they, Samuel?"

"Just how they should be. You and me. That's all."

The Max Bruch *Concerto No. 1 for Violin and Orchestra* had progressed to the final movement. Adam, as the featured violinist for the concerto, had played confidently and with great feeling. This was the first time Frances and Samuel had seen him perform in a solo piece and they were impressed. But it was here, in the energetic final stages, that his eyes locked upon Frances. Hypnotised, she found it impossible to look away as she watched his hand guide the bow across the strings. His movements were persuasive, masterful, sensual, as he appeared to stroke the belly of the violin that arched slightly towards him.

He looked at her across the violin. With each movement of his hand across the bridge with the bow, he imagined he was stroking her, making love to her. This was a woman who loved music. This was a woman who had feelings. And she wasn't married to Samuel.

Frances pushed at a pulse beating rapidly in her throat. There was a warm tingling spreading through her that was unfamiliar.

The music, his eyes, his hands, captured her. Tantalized her. Aroused her. She had never allowed herself to be aroused before; she felt frightened and confused. Panic seized her and she half-rose from her seat. Samuel turned towards Frances, putting a hand on her arm.

"What is it?" he whispered into her ear.

She shook her head, then slumped back into her seat. The last few notes rose from Adam's violin without fault, although he had been watching Frances closely, and the concerto was at an end. Fervent acclaim from the audience shattered Frances's fear, bringing her back to reality and awareness of those around her. A hot flush of perspiration took her by surprise and she wondered briefly if she had a temperature.

The ride back to Frances's apartment had been a heavily silent one with her refusal to discuss her behaviour. Feeling not a little piqued, Samuel sulked with the impression that she was excluding him, and their parting was quite strained. When she inserted her key into the lock of the security door of her apartment building, she turned to wave as usual to Samuel, but was surprised to find that he had already driven off.

"I wonder what's wrong with him?" she mumbled to herself as she closed the door behind her.

The morning had been busy with a steady stream of customers, leaving very little time for any discussion between Frances and Samuel. He had the feeling that she was taking every opportunity to avoid talking to him, but he wanted to clear the air so that things could return to normal. He wondered if he'd done anything to offend her but, after much soul-searching, decided that his behaviour had been exemplary. *It's Harcourt*, he scowled inwardly. *I'm sure of it.*

Just before the lunchtime rush, they had time to grab a coffee and sit for a few minutes in the *Poet's Corner*. Samuel bulldozed his way into the subject of Adam.

"He's after you. I can tell."

"I wish you'd stop that," Frances said crossly.

"He's fascinated by you."

"I hardly think so."

He watched her carefully before going on. "I think you like him too."

"He's a nice man," she conceded as she pretended interest in a pile of books on the coffee table before them. "A talented musician."

"Is that all?"

"Yes," she said deliberately, looking straight at him. "That's all."

He smiled. "This is Samuel you're talking to. I know how you think."

Her eyes blazed. "No you don't, Samuel." She leaned forward, tapping him on the knee. "No you don't."

"I see how you look at him," he persisted.

"Will you drop it please?"

"It's just that I worry about you." His tone was petulant.

"Why would my talking to Adam worry you? Tell me that."

"It worries me because I'm afraid you'll get hurt."

"Hurt? By whom?"

"By Adam."

"What are you talking about?"

"If you get close to him. A relationship."

"Will you get this through your thick head. I have no intentions of having a close relationship with anyone." She stood up with a pile of books in her arms. "Least of all Adam."

"Huh!"

"What do you mean, huh?"

"Nothing."

"Now you're sulking."

"I'm not. If you won't talk about it…"

"There's nothing to talk about." She began shelving the books.

"It's just that…I care about you…what happens to you. I'd hate to see someone take advantage of you."

"I know you care about me," she smiled down at him. "But I'm a big girl. I can look after myself. There's nothing to worry about."

He sighed. "I'd miss you."

"Miss me? Why on earth…?"

"If you married."

"Married! What…?"

"Well, what if you married Adam, for argument's sake, and left *The Bookcase*—I'd never see you again."

Frances put the remaining books on a shelf and sat down beside him. "Is that what this is about?" she asked gently.

"You'd be throwing away all that we've worked for."

"I'm not about to throw anything away…least of all," she gestured around the shop, "…this. Look—I'm not about to get married. Not now. Not ever!"

"You might one day."

"No—but what if I did? Do you think our friendship means that little to me? That I'd forget about you?" She kissed him on the cheek. "I love you. You and the shop are the best things that've happened to me."

Samuel returned the kiss, looking relieved.

She rose to her feet and continued to shelve the books. She muttered more to herself than to him, "No one…nothing…could ever change that."

Chapter 9

Lunchtime proved to be as busy as Frances and Samuel had expected. They spent the rest of the afternoon tidying up *The Bookcase* and re-shelving books in between attending to customers. Frances was perched on the top rung of a small ladder, taking books that Samuel handed her, when the doorbell rang.

They turned to see Adam enter the shop. He looked different in casual clothes—more relaxed, Frances thought. There was a momentary silence.

"Frances?" Adam was incredulous. "Samuel?"

"Adam!" She remained frozen on the ladder.

"What are you doing here?" Samuel asked rather rudely.

"My God," he said, looking around the shop, "this is *your* book shop!" Adam hit his forehead. "I should have known."

Samuel leaned against the wall nonchalantly. "Were you looking for us?"

"No. I was looking for *The Bookcase* not realising that it was yours. It comes highly recommended."

"How nice!" Frances said, climbing down from the ladder. Adam took advantage of the situation in offering her his hand and she took it gingerly. Her heart raced at the contact.

"How long have you owned it?" he asked, looking from one to the other.

"Well, it used to be my parents' business," Samuel explained, "but my father became ill some ten years back and couldn't continue."

"Oh, I see."

"I was only too willing to give up my accountancy practice to take it on. I didn't know enough about the literary world, though, and that's where Frances came in."

"Samuel enticed me away from the State Library where I was working."

"And it's her expertise in books that has made *The Bookcase* so successful."

"What nonsense!" She turned to Adam. "What is it you're looking for?"

"I've been trying for some time to get an out-of-print edition on Paganini."

"Well, you've come to the right person, Adam," Samuel chipped in proudly, putting aside his hostility for the moment. He was a businessman through and through and when he saw the opportunity for a sale, he waxed enthusiasm. "Frances can help you if anyone can."

"I can only try," she blushed. "What's the title?"

"Well, that's the problem. I don't know the title. You remember I mentioned that elderly blind lady I used to read to?"

"Yes, you told us she gave you your first violin."

"That's right. Well, she had this particular book and I used to read bits of it out to her. That's another reason I became interested in violins. Well, after she died, all of her effects disappeared when her estate was wound up. She'd left the book to me, but I don't know what happened to it. I was only a kid, you see."

"And you don't remember any part of the title?" Frances moved towards the music section as she spoke.

"No. Afraid not. It was very old though. I've asked for it in so many book shops but no one seems to know anything about it."

She ran her fingers along the rows of books, searching the titles with her eyes, then she stopped as a thought struck her. "Adam, I don't know if it's the same book, but I have a very old one—a collector's item—about Paganini. It belonged to my father. He's a violinist, like yourself."

"Is he? I didn't realise."

"Yes. And my mother's a pianist." She looked down at the floor and added quietly, "They are very fine musicians."

"I might know them! What are their names?"

"Eleanor and Robert Draper."

"But of course! I've seen them perform—years ago, mind you. They're wonderful musicians. You must be very proud."

She nodded, shrugging. "Ahhh...yes."

"They travelled a lot, didn't they, especially around Europe. Are they still performing?"

"I don't really know."

"Oh?" Adam looked quizzically at Frances. There was an uncomfortable pause. He changed the subject, wondering what he'd said. "And your father gave you the book, you said?"

"Yes. He thought it might encourage me to play the violin, but I'm afraid I didn't inherit their musical ability."

"I wonder if it's the same book?"

"You're welcome to borrow it, if it is. And in the meantime, I can try to get a copy for you, if any exist today."

"That'd be terrific!"

"I hope I'll be able to get it for you."

"It's very good of you to lend me yours."

"I'm sure you'll look after it."

He held his hand over his heart. "With my life, mademoiselle!"

She hesitated. "It's at my place. The book, I mean."

"Can I pick it up sometime?"

Her words came out in a rush. "You can get it today, if you like."

Neither of them saw the frown that crept across Samuel's face. "How?"

"Well, we're about to close up in..." she looked at her watch, "...another fifteen minutes. I live just over on the other side of the park. You could go back with me—have a coffee if you'd like." *What am I saying?*

"I'd like that very much."

The quivering at the corners of his mouth had started again. It fascinated her. She dragged her eyes away to find his eyes smiling into hers; it was hard not to respond.

"That's settled then," she smiled back, surprising herself. "If it's the book you're looking for, you can take it with you."

"Frances, I can't thank you enough!"

She suddenly became conscious of the fact that Samuel had been left out of the conversation, and turned to him. "Coming too, Samuel?"

"Wouldn't miss it for the world," he replied dryly.

The walk through the Fitzroy Gardens had been tense for Frances as she berated herself inwardly for putting herself in the position of having to entertain Adam, albeit just to look for the book and a coffee. *I could have brought the book into the shop and he could have picked it up from there!* She was grateful that Samuel had agreed to accompany them, but at the same time she was a little annoyed at his obvious sarcasm. She suspected he was jealous of Adam and wished she could convince him that his fears were groundless. She knew they were groundless—of course! *Adam's just a nice man. That's all.*

Samuel had the opportunity, though, to show off his knowledge of plant life and birds, and he kept the conversation going throughout most of their walk, pointing out interesting facts of both species. Adam proved an attentive listener, stopping at various points to ask Samuel the names of certain plants. They chatted easily with Frances watching them, wishing she could thaw out her mind and tongue. *I'm never like this.*

A sparrow hopped along the gravel path in front of Frances as if to dare her to catch up with it. Its little head twitched around and looked up at her as she neared it. Then it twittered and flew up into the air, circled around her and then landed in front of her again until she got too close.

"Cheeky!" Frances laughed at it.

"What's that?" Samuel asked, as he and Adam paused in their conversation.

"That sparrow. I could swear it was teasing me."

"The common house sparrow—in actual fact, they're Old World Weaver Finches," Samuel recited. "The most abundant songbird in the world—and the biggest pest."

"Oh, they're sweet!" Frances protested. "And I'm sure this one knows me."

"Don't they all?" Adam asked. "I mean, if you walk through here every day, I'm sure they'd all want to be your friend—like in the Disney movies."

"Now you're teasing me," she smiled.

Adam and Samuel were out on the balcony looking over the gardens when Frances called from the lounge room. "Coffee's ready."

The men took their mugs and sat down, Samuel lounging comfortably on the sofa beside Frances and Adam taking an armchair. He picked up a large book from the coffee table.

"I can't believe it," he said, leafing through the book slowly. "I've looked for it for so long."

"Well, it's yours for as long as you like," Frances smiled.

"Are you sure? I feel a bit nervous borrowing it."

"No need. And I'll start the hunt for your own copy tomorrow."

"Thank you so much."

They looked at each other for a long moment. Samuel broke the silence with a cough and Frances looked down at her coffee mug.

"Any more coffee, dear?" Samuel asked.

"Yes. Yes, of course." She jumped up and hurried to the kitchen, where she put the empty plunger down with shaking hands. *Stop it!* She leaned against the bench as she waited for the kettle to boil. The murmur of the men's voices was just discernible over a CD playing in the background. She wondered what they were talking about—if Samuel was being rude. He'd been like his old self in the gardens but now that they'd arrived in her apartment, he seemed caustic again. *He's not usually this unpredictable.* Pouring boiling water onto the coffee grounds, she inhaled the aroma. *Get a hold of yourself*, she scolded, as she made a few attempts at holding the plunger without shaking. *Deep breaths.* She inhaled, closing her eyes, concentrating on calming herself.

"Need any help?" Adam's voice behind her made her jump.

"Pardon?"

"Can I carry that for you?"

"Yes, thanks," she said, thrusting the plunger at him.

She felt jittery standing so close to him, and she noticed that the corners of his mouth were quivering.

"Are you laughing at me?" she demanded suddenly.

"No," he laughed. "Why?"

"You look like you're about to fall over in a fit."

He smiled broadly. "Would you like me to?"

"Silly."

He followed her into the lounge room.

Samuel looked up at them. "Ah, good. The coffee!"

Adam looked out of the french doors. "How fortunate you are to live so close to your work."

"Yes, that's one of the major reasons why I chose this apartment," Frances said.

"Where do you live, Adam?" Samuel asked, holding out his mug to Frances.

"I've got a house in Mornington."

Frances looked up. "What a long way to travel to work!"

"It's becoming a nightmare," Adam agreed.

Samuel grimaced. "I can imagine."

"I'm in the city nearly every night of the week. All I seem to do is drive, perform, drive."

"Why don't you move closer to the city?" Frances asked as she sat back on the sofa beside Samuel.

"Perhaps he likes the country life, dear."

"It's just not practical anymore," Adam shook his head.

"It'd drive me mad," Frances said.

"It does. Especially in the winter months."

"Oh, I don't know." Samuel said between sips of coffee. "There's a lot to be said for country life. You can't get work closer to home?"

Frances frowned at him. "Don't be ridiculous!"

"Afraid not," Adam said. "I'll have to do something about it soon though."

Chapter 10

Frances sits with Plato high up on a broad branch of a tree amongst the canopy. The sun filters through the leaves and onto Plato's fur which ripples as her fingers stroke it. She sees Adam standing below, looking up at her. She smiles as he begins to play his violin. It is the Vivaldi *Four Seasons*, the *Summer* adagio. It is peaceful here as she listens to the soft, gentle hum of summer sounds until the frenzy of cellos herald the wind and storms of the finale. She threatens to lose her balance on the branch as Plato suddenly changes to the shape of an indistinct man. The storm of *Summer* is replaced by the furious animation of the Dukas *Sorcerer's Apprentice*. The indistinct man pushes Frances off the branch to where Adam takes on the aspect of a devil with pointed ears. The corners of his mouth quiver into a leering grin. Fangs protrude from his thick, wet lips. The twisted roots of a giant fig tree rise up over her head, squeezing her in on all sides, pulsating with the crashes of the music. She screams as the roots close up over her.

She awoke screaming, gasping for breath, perspiration soaking her hair and nightgown. Plato's paws dug into her stomach through the sheet as he looked at her with radiant eyes. Frances sat up suddenly and turned on her bedside lamp. The room sprung starkly into view, banishing the memory of the nightmare and the fear that it engendered, shredding it away into the darkness outside. Her fearful mind made no effort to follow it, to dredge it up and turn it over to examine it, to try to understand it. Rather, she turned her attention to Plato, talking softly to him, stroking him, as she curled into the foetal position trying to summon sleep.

The rest of the night, Frances tossed in an uneasy doze, until she gave up and made a strong black coffee. She drank it sitting on her balcony watching the sun rise over the city buildings, reluctantly wondering about the nightmare which lingered in her mind. There was something about the giant tree that tugged at her memory but she couldn't grasp it.

A long hot shower relaxed her tight, weary body. She dried herself vigorously before bending over to touch her toes twenty times, as she did every morning. Colour tinged her pale cheeks with the sudden rush of blood.

"That looks better," she told her reflection.

She chose a black pants suit with a pale green silk blouse. A pair of emerald earrings complemented the blouse, as did a matching brooch that she pinned on the lapel of her jacket.

A packet of muesli stood on the kitchen bench where she had put it before deciding to feed Plato. He looked up at her and meowed impatiently as she emptied a portion of meat into his bowl.

"Starving as usual, I see," she smiled, as she bent down to place the bowl on the floor. He buried his nose into the bowl enthusiastically.

She stood up and looked at the packet of muesli, then put it back in the pantry untouched.

"See you later," she said, bending down to stroke Plato. "You be a good boy, eh?"

She let herself out of the apartment, looking up at the sky, glad she wouldn't need her umbrella. Crossing Albert Street she began her walk along the usual path to *The Bookcase*. She turned instead onto another path, one which avoided the large fig tree near the River God fountain, and found herself passing the Temple of the Winds. Inside it, a young woman leaned against one of the Corinthian columns, whilst her lover, holding her arms behind her, kissed her passionately. Both dressed in white, they might have been ancients visiting a temple built for them. Frances's steps slowed as she watched them for a long moment until they looked up and saw her. They grinned and then put on a show for her, exaggerating their ardour.

"Want to join us?" the young man called out. His companion giggled before pulling his head down to her mouth again.

Embarrassed, she hurried past them, finding it difficult to breathe normally, not wanting them to see the blush spreading up to her face. She strode out blindly, knocking into a jogger who was passing from the opposite direction.

"Sorry," they both said at the same time.

She continued along another path which took her past a row of fig trees. Half-hidden by the large cavernous roots, another pair of lovers were in a close embrace. She saw a glimpse of naked thigh where the man's hand had pulled up the woman's skirt. The woman's fingers pulled at the fabric of her lover's T-shirt, freeing it from his jeans. She raked at his back as their bodies pushed together in their urgency for each other, blissfully unaware of their audience. Frances recoiled from the scene, running wildly down the path, until a stitch slowed her steps. She looked longingly at a park bench, her feet aching from the unaccustomed flight in high heels, but she felt the need to get out of the gardens and enter the safety of work.

Walking quickly along the central path, she arrived at Clarendon Street at what seemed like hours after she had left her apartment. Her watch showed that only seven minutes had passed since she'd entered the gardens. She stood looking at *The Bookcase* for some time before crossing the road, waiting for her breathing to slow and to smooth out her ruffled feathers.

Samuel was already inside *The Bookcase*, opening his briefcase in the back room. He wore a new navy blue suit and waited for Frances to comment about it, along with the bright red and blue patterned tie he'd just checked in the mirror. She always noticed anything new he wore.

"Lovely morning," he said expectantly, as Frances put her handbag down.

"Yes," she replied noncommittally.

The rest of the morning passed by quickly enough with stock arriving and a steady stream of customers. Samuel was occupied in *Poet's Corner* with an elderly woman needing help with the choosing of books for her grandchildren. They sat in the armchairs discussing the merits of classic children's story writers versus modern Australian writers. A large pile of books was heaped upon the coffee table.

"I do appreciate your time," the woman beamed at him.

Samuel oozed an easy charm that never failed to put people at their ease. He radiated patience, an all-absorbing interest in whatever they had to say, and invariably won them over with a sale. He was genuine, though—a natural salesman.

Frances handed her customer a gift-wrapped book and the receipt.

"I hope he'll be happy with it," she smiled.

"It seems just the sort of thing he would like," the customer smiled back. "You never fail to choose just the right book for him."

"I'm glad."

The customer left the shop and Frances turned to a young man of about twenty years of age. He was unshaven, appeared not to have combed his hair that day, and had obviously been drinking even at such an early hour. Frances's nostrils curled despite herself at the smell of stale beer. She hoped he hadn't noticed, but he seemed busy trying to balance the books he'd chosen in one arm and getting his wallet out of a tight trouser pocket with the other hand.

"Here, let me take them," she said, putting the books on the counter in front of her.

He winked at her.

"Will that be all, sir?"

"Good shop, this," he smirked.

"Thank you."

He looked her up and down, standing on his toes to look over the counter at her legs. "Nice staff, too."

"Was there something else?" she asked coldly, as she began ringing up the price of the books on the cash register.

He looked down at his pocket, still struggling with the wallet which had caught on a seam. He lurched around the side of the counter, losing his balance, ending up close to Frances. She shrunk well away from him, trembling.

"Samuel," she called over to him, trying to keep her voice calm. "Can you take care of this?"

"Why, yes," he answered, surprised. "Is there a problem?"

"No. Just finish this sale, would you?"

He looked at her in puzzlement but refrained from comment. He apologised to the woman he'd been assisting, assuring her he would return immediately.

"Certainly," he said smoothly, taking over. "Now that's forty-two ninety-five, sir. Is there anything else?"

Frances walked out to the back of the shop, leaving Samuel with the young man. Waves of nausea and sudden perspiration had her trembling. She sat down with a glass of cold water.

"You look a bit shaken," Samuel said quietly, joining her. "Did he say something to upset you?"

"That smell…" she gasped, "…he stank of beer!"

"There's no law against beer. Would you have rathered he smelt of champagne?"

"It's not funny! He was revolting."

"He may be that, but why are you so upset?" He touched her on the arm. "My God, you're shaking!"

"I'm all right."

"You don't look it."

Frances failed to respond as she shut her eyes and leaned back against her chair. He glanced back to *Poet's Corner*, relieved to see the woman leafing through the books he'd shown her.

"Look, if he comes in again, I'll take care of him. Keep him away from you."

He noticed how pale Frances was. Her eyes were open again, but they were glazed. There was no expression on her face as she stared straight in front of her. He wasn't sure how to handle the situation as he bent over to look at her closely. He waved a hand before her face.

"Hello? The lights have gone out."

Her eyes blinked and she sighed deeply. She looked puzzled.

"What happened there? Where were you?"

"I think I'm going to be sick."

She clamped her hand over her mouth and rushed into the bathroom, banging the door behind her. Samuel looked after her in amazement.

Chapter 11

A week later found Frances and Samuel in their usual seats in the front row of the concert hall. The lights dimmed as the orchestra waited, eyes on the conductor, waiting for his signal to begin. Someone coughed over the expectant hush and the conductor's baton hesitated for an instant before his arm described an arc in the air.

Adam's hand guided the bow unwaveringly across the strings during Mendelssohn's big orchestral work where he, as the soloist, participated from the start in the virtuoso display piece. The violin concerto captivated the audience as the melody flowed into receptive ears. She was captivated by Adam as she watched his deft movements, the way his powerful frame filled his clothes, the way he stood solidly as if nothing could ever knock him from his place. The light played around his face, deepening the dimple. It picked up lights in his hair, and she wondered if it was soft, what it smelled like, if he used hair spray, how often he washed it. *Does he shave before he goes on stage?*

She pulled herself up with a start, concentrating on the music again.

He knew she'd been studying him as his eyes met hers from time to time during the performance. Every time, though, her gaze bounced away from him as if she were afraid. *Afraid of what?* She was there, threatening his concentration, and he closed his eyes to shut her out, but not before he noticed her eyes glaze. He realised she was lost in the music and another world. He saw the shimmer of tears and knew that she was crying.

Robert Draper stands before his wife as she watches him play the Mendelssohn concerto. He plays for her, and no one else. Her head is tilted up towards him as she sits on a chair from where her royal blue velvet dress cascades in thick furrows. Frances clutches her teddy bear in her arms as she stands in the doorway. She wants to sit on her mother's knee amongst the soft velvet, and be closer to the perfume that she can smell. Her mother notices her and waves her away with annoyance. Tears pour down Frances's face as she pleads to stay, to watch her father. Her mother raises her hand, index finger pointed stiffly towards the staircase. Her eyes are hard, like diamonds—unforgiving. Frances hugs her teddy bear to her as she climbs the staircase slowly.

Frances escaped her memories and returned to the concerto where Adam's hand, clutching his violin, replaced that of her father's. She was surprised, yet again, to find that her face was wet with tears and she blotted them furtively.

As the concerto ended, and the musicians began to leave the stage, Adam tried to catch her eye. He was fascinated by what he thought was her reaction to the music and wondered if each concert she attended was an ordeal for her. *Why would she come if it was*, he asked himself. She talked about classical music as if it was one of her life's greatest pleasures, and she attended concerts often with Samuel. So why would she cry like that? If it was sheer emotion—being carried by the beauty of the music—then why would she look so miserable? He wished he could ask her sometime but sensed that it would be a subject difficult to broach.

Samuel remained totally unaware of what Frances was going through. When he settled down to listen to a concert, he quite often closed his eyes to take the music in, to concentrate without the distraction of the movements of the musicians. So by the time each concert was finished, Frances had had time to compose herself and replace her emotional scars with the cool mask that she was so adept at creating.

Adam drove home slowly, deep in thought. He had sworn never to have anything to do with another woman—any woman—but Frances was getting under his skin. His thoughts constantly returned to her—when he practised, when he ran along the beach in the early hours of the morning, when he lay in bed at night. The old bitterness of his wife's betrayal seemed less painful somehow. And for the first time in a long while he admitted to himself that he was lonely.

When he pulled into the driveway of his weatherboard cottage on Mornington's Esplanade, he wished that for once there was a welcoming light to make coming home worthwhile. Having someone waiting for him, or arriving with someone he was close to, would inject life into the neglected little cottage. Not for the first time, he considered his mother's entreaties to return to the family home in Portarlington. It was certainly an attractive offer—being back amongst the noisy camaraderie that he shared with his brothers—but he knew it would be the death of his career.

Although the night was cold, the sky was cloudless with a bright moon reflecting a silver radiance on the calm waters of the bay. He drew the fresh, crisp air into his lungs and decided to walk along Fisherman's Beach. Crossing the road, he made his way down a path cut through the scrub and stopped close to the water's edge. The soft whisper of the flat, rippling waves was broken by an occasional cry of a night bird, and the quick thrum of a car's motor as it drove past on the Esplanade above him. With his hands deep in his pockets, he trudged along to the far left curve of the beach, then turned back to walk in the opposite direction.

In the summer he loved it here in the early hours of the morning when he jogged until perspiration dripped from every pore and then enjoyed an invigorating swim in the salty water. He would then run up the path, cross the Esplanade and have a quick shower before having some breakfast.

Fugue

When he first moved to Mornington, three months after Melanie walked out of their flat in Hawthorn, it was a relief to return home from work without the overwhelming guilt of having left her alone at night, and to read the morning newspaper without being screamed at. And there was the luxury of being able to set up a music room without the fear of having sheet music moved and instruments handled roughly—all in the cause of tidiness. But when he entered the house, it seemed to echo loneliness from every room. The untidy but clean clutter showed that a musician lived there, but not very often. If an inventory had been taken of the contents of the pantry and the refrigerator, a month later not much would have been consumed or replaced.

He often thought, with regret, how little chance he had to spend more time there, to look out over the bay whilst listening to a new CD, pick the fruit that dropped from the various fruit trees that surrounded the house, plant some seedlings in the garden, get to know the neighbours. But the constant travelling to and from work, as well as the private music lessons he gave to young children in the neighbourhood, took up most of what time he had. Without being conscious of his reasons, Adam gave as much to his young pupils as his blind mentor, Mrs Lindberg, had given him when he was a child. They liked Adam's knack of sympathetic communication, his patience, his easy-going manner, all of which made him an effective teacher. Adam enjoyed his contact with the young eager children, and he missed their excited babble when they left to return to their own homes. Their mothers would thank him with anxious questions about their children's progress, and keep the handsome violinist talking as long as they could, wondering about him and why he was alone. He'd often thought about having children of his own. It was something he'd always expected, coming from a large family; his brothers already had an even dozen between them. Melanie had refused point-blank to have children. She didn't want her perfect figure pushed out of shape by "little snotty-nosed brats", as she'd called them. "Don't expect me to stay home looking after your little horrors while you're out having a good time every night." The fact that he was performing in concerts and earning a living for them didn't seem to impact upon her. He eventually became accustomed to the idea of a childless marriage and the disappointed faces of his parents as their eldest son failed to provide them with more grandchildren.

Adam walked back up his driveway and let himself into the house. He walked through the rooms without turning on light switches, the moon's luminescence casting enough light for him to see by. He flopped into a large leather armchair beside an empty fire place, curiously awake, his mind a riot of images. Melanie's angry face flitted in and out of his head, the memory of her shrill voice almost discernible in the silent house. Then an image of a pair of deep-brown, tearful eyes set in a pale, beautiful face intruded again, pushing Melanie back into the closed recesses where she belonged, and he found himself fantasizing about what a little girl would look like if she belonged to Frances and him.

He shook his head, amused at himself, clearing the notion from his mind as his eyes lit upon a pile of folders on the floor containing sheet music. He sighed as he thought of the composing that had come to an abrupt halt with Melanie's condemnation, his dreams tucked inside the folders that hadn't been opened for years. *One day...*

Chapter 12

Poet's Corner was jam-packed, Samuel holding court over a gathering of university students. The heated arguments made Frances smile to herself as she attended to customers who were unfamiliar with the camaraderie shared between Samuel and his devotees.

"You're most welcome to join them," she assured a young man as he pocketed his change.

He looked doubtful. "Oh, I don't know…"

"No, really. They'd love another point of view." She led the way over to the group. "And I can get you a coffee."

"You've twisted my arm," the man said.

"Good! Let me introduce you to everyone."

A place was eagerly made for the newcomer and he was quickly drawn into the discussion. Frances took orders for refills and busied herself in the back room making more coffee. As she returned with a tray of steaming hot mugs, the doorbell rang. Everyone looked up to see if it was someone they knew.

Adam entered the shop looking a little uncomfortable with a bunch of flowers in his hand and all eyes upon him.

"Adam!" Frances blushed her pleasure at seeing him.

"Are they for me?" Samuel called over to him.

"I don't think they're your shade," Adam pulled a face, then laughed.

The group burst into laughter and indicated noisily that he should join them.

He held up his hands. "Sorry, I don't have that long."

"Next time, then," Samuel called out good-naturedly.

Adam held out the flowers to Frances. "A thank you. For the book."

"Oh, there's no need…"

"Yes there is. I'm grateful."

She took the flowers, inhaling their perfume.

"And I thought I'd have a bit more of a look around this time," he added, looking at his watch.

"Would you like some help?"

"Great!"

"You'd probably like the arts section. We've quite a good selection on the composers."

They wandered over to the shelves where they spoke quietly, their voices being drowned by the resumed discussion in *Poet's Corner*. Samuel was a little quieter, at first, as he kept a wary eye on Frances and Adam, but he was soon dragged back into an argument. He shrugged, turning his attention away from them.

"I'd love to stay longer," Adam smiled at her, "and join in the discussion." He looked in the direction of the others. "They seem to be having a ball."

"It gets very lively at times," she said. "Almost too lively."

"Well, I'd better get going," he grimaced. "Rehearsals."

He paid for two books that he'd chosen and she saw him to the door.

"Are you and Samuel going to the Saturday night concert?"

"Is it the Tchaikovsky?"

"Yes…the sixth."

"Oh, yes. We'll be there. I wouldn't miss it for the world!"

"How about coffee after?" He rushed on. "You and Samuel, I mean."

"That'd be lovely."

"I'll look forward to it."

"And thank you for the flowers." She blushed.

"Entirely my pleasure."

She retrieved the flowers from the counter, bending over them to inhale the perfume again. She was unaware that the roses reflected their crimson colour onto her face as if she'd blushed. Samuel caught her eye as she turned to make her way to the back of the shop with the flowers, and she was surprised at the frown upon his face. *What's wrong with him?*

The crystal vase complemented the roses perfectly and she stood back to admire her arrangement before taking them out to put on the counter in the public space where everyone could enjoy them. She felt rather pleased because Samuel was usually the only person who gave her flowers, except for her friend, Gail. She smiled at the memory of her last birthday when Gail had surprised her with a bonsai tree.

"It's a Snow Rose Serissa—from Japan," Gail had told her proudly. "It's supposed to flower ten months of the year!"

"It's absolutely gorgeous," Frances had enthused, admiring the miniature white rose-shaped flowers that grew in profusion over the tiny plant.

As a rule, Gail presented Frances with an enormous arrangement of flowers for her birthday, and Frances was curious as to why she gave her the bonsai this time.

"So that you always have it," Gail had explained, "and that you always have flowers. They die in a vase after a few days but this won't as long as you look after it."

"I've always wanted a bonsai," Frances had exclaimed. "How did you know?"

"You told me."

"When?"

"When I did the composite resin restoration on your lower left cuspid."

"Pardon?"

"That's a tooth," Gail grinned. "In your mouth."

"How on earth…?"

"That one," she tapped the top of a tooth in her own mouth.

"But that was ages ago."

"So?"

"And I never get a chance to say anything. You've always got my mouth full!"

"Ah, but I know what you'd like to say."

"Gail," Frances laughed, "sometimes I think you're a magician."

On the following Saturday night, *Parklands Restaurant* was surprisingly full for the hour of night when Frances entered with Adam and Samuel.

"The sign of a popular restaurant," Samuel observed. "They've done well since they opened."

Adam had changed out of his concert dress into a pair of dark brown trousers with a soft green shirt under a tweed jacket. He carried his violin case with him and placed it beside his feet when they sat down at a table. Their waiter offered to look after it for Adam, but he declined.

"Too valuable to give other people the responsibility," he explained to Frances and Samuel. "I'm never game enough to leave it in the boot of my car either."

They ordered coffee and liqueurs and settled into a conversation regarding Adam's visit to *The Bookcase*.

"I've read about a third of the Stradivari biography," he said. "You were right—it is a more comprehensive one than others I've read."

Frances was pleased. "I thought you'd enjoy it."

"I'm glad you suggested it. And the one on Egyptian Mythology…"

"The one for your mother?"

"Yes. She was thrilled with it."

"I'm so glad!"

"She's always been fascinated with ancient Egypt. She's sorry she never went there."

"It's not too late, is it?"

"She thinks so."

"How old is she?"

"Sixty five yesterday," he said, taking a sip of coffee. "Says it's too late for her to travel that far."

"Surely not!"

"She wouldn't go on her own—and Dad's not interested."

"Couldn't you go with her?"

"I've suggested that, but I think she'd take a bit of persuading."

Samuel sat back watching the two, feeling a little left out. His eyes narrowed as he saw the way Adam looked at Frances, and how animated she was in her reaction to him. He sulked as unreasonable pangs of jealousy pulled at him. *She never looks at me like that*, he thought peevishly. Then he smiled inwardly at himself. *If she did look at me like that, I'd be in real trouble!* He signalled to the waiter for more liqueurs and, as he did so, Frances realised that he hadn't been a part of the conversation. She put her hand on his arm.

"Samuel's been to Egypt, haven't you?"

"Oh, have you?" Adam looked at Samuel with interest.

"Yes."

"When was that?"

"In the seventies."

"What did you think of it?"

"Fascinating."

Samuel's pique was obvious from his short answers and there was an uncomfortable silence.

Frances cleared her throat and said brightly, "Well, I hope you can persuade your mother, Adam."

"Yes, I hope so." He paused. "Have you ever been there?"

"No. I'd love to go, though."

Adam smiled. "Perhaps you might come with Mum and me one day?" His eyes teased her.

"I doubt that very much," Samuel said stiffly.

"Oh?" Adam looked at him carefully. "Why?"

"She's too busy in the shop." Samuel's reply was clipped. "But we might shut it up for a month some time—or get a manager—and go together."

Frances looked at Samuel in surprise, then her jaw firmed defiantly. She refrained, though, from commenting, not wishing to cause an argument, although she seethed underneath. Adam noticed the tightness of her jaw and raised an eyebrow wordlessly. Samuel wondered if he'd pushed her too far.

During a quiet time in *The Bookcase* the following day, Frances and Samuel had a chance to sit over a coffee in the *Poet's Corner*.

"I didn't mean anything by it," he said defensively.

"I just don't understand your antagonism towards Adam."

"I'm not antagonistic!"

"Yes you are!" She stabbed a finger at him in the air. "And he's only ever been charming to us."

"To you," he sulked.

"There you go again." Her voice rose in anger. "If I didn't know better, I'd say you were jealous."

"Jealous? Me?"

"Yes."

There was a momentary pause as they regarded each other.

"Well, I suppose I am a bit," he conceded.

"But why?"

"It's just that we've been so close for so long. He's coming between us."

The anger left her. "Oh, Samuel, dear. As if anyone could come between us."

She leaned over to pat his hand when the doorbell rang.

"I'll get it," she said.

He stayed in the armchair, fingering his coffee mug, deep in thought. It seemed like his comfortable world was being tipped over the edge, exposing raw undersides that he'd hoped he would never see again. He watched Frances attend to their customer. *What would I do without her*, he wondered for the umpteenth time. *The shop would suffer and so would I.*

He had to admit to himself that since he'd told Philip he'd asked Frances to marry him, their relationship had taken a turn for the worse. He realised he'd been insensitive, expecting Philip to accept just one more aspect of the terms of their association—terms that he'd mostly set. In the nine years since they'd first met, Philip had reluctantly agreed to keeping their relationship private—not that he had a problem with his own sexuality—due to Samuel's obsession with keeping it from his parents and the rest of his circle of friends and work acquaintances. But when Frances had appeared on the scene Samuel's cover had seemed complete, and Philip had realised that any chance of Samuel's *coming out* was very remote. Any notion of Philip and Samuel living together had always been smoothly pushed to one side and Samuel had very little idea of how that had affected his partner. Until he asked Frances to marry him.

Samuel grimaced as he remembered the scene with Philip. It hadn't been easy to convince him to continue with their association, or to erase the hurt from his eyes. It seemed like he was under pressure from all sides, and he hated himself for jeopardizing the only true relationship he'd ever been lucky enough to hang onto. He knew he'd been selfish and he was ashamed. But how could he satisfy the desire of his parents for grandchildren, the needs of his lover, and still keep Frances for himself?

Chapter 13

Samuel frowned as he looked down at his programme. The arched right eyebrow on Bach's fleshy, full-lipped face, framed a piercing look of disapproval at Samuel, as if to say: "Get a hold of yourself, man." *That's all right for you*, Samuel grimaced back at the bewigged composer.

The energy of the violin concerto failed to ease him out of his blackening frame of mind. From the corner of his eye he watched Frances sitting forward, her lips parted, breathing quickly. *She's aroused*, Samuel thought grimly as he switched to her point of focus. Adam was smiling at her as he played. *How does he do that? Why doesn't he make a mistake!*

The rest of the programme before interval was lost on Samuel as his thoughts whirled in a jealous fog. He was unable to concentrate on the music with his normal deep involvement. Even shutting his eyes didn't work as the image of Frances's reaction to Adam lay tattooed on his eyelid.

I don't care what she says, that man'll come between us!

Samuel looked with misgiving into his champagne flute; the cold bubbling liquid tasted sour in his mouth. The conversation between them was stilted, sparse. He knew she was looking for Adam as her eyes searched the crowd in vain. She drank unconsciously, taking little sips often. She tried to look surreptitiously over her shoulder but Samuel distracted her.

"You've finished your drink already," he feigned surprise. "You must have been thirsty."

"Yes, I suppose so."

"Do you want mine?" he offered.

"Why?" She looked at him in surprise. "Don't you want it?"

"No, I think you need it more than me."

Frances took the offered glass without comment, her attention being drawn back to the crowded foyer. A hardly noticeable frown skimmed across her features when the bell rang calling the audience back to its seats. Her eyes reflected concern as she looked back at the sea of faces that failed to produce whom she was looking for.

"Coming?" Samuel's voice was tinged with causticity.

"Yes. Yes," she smiled, forcing the disappointment from her voice. Her face was a mask of fabricated poise.

They made their way along the carpeted aisle and returned to their seats. Samuel watched her fidgety movements as she pretended interest in the programme.

"So," he said. "This should be good, eh?"

"What?"

"The symphony," he said slowly. "That's what we're here for, in case you don't remember."

She raised an eyebrow. "No need to be sarcastic," she snapped.

He held up his hands in mock surrender. "Sorry. I didn't realise you were so touchy tonight."

"I'm not touchy," she retorted.

"Huh!"

A woman seated next to Frances glanced at her and Samuel curiously. He sat back in his seat, crossing his legs, and glared at the stage in front of him.

Just then Adam walked onto the stage and bowed to the audience. As he did so, he smiled down at Frances. *She looks relieved,* Samuel thought, as her mouth softened into a returning smile. Her whole body seemed to sag into her seat. The lights dimmed and the symphony began. For the first time since he had known Frances, Samuel was aware of the tears that she shed during the performance. He was puzzled by them. Was she upset with him?

Had he been too sarcastic? Had his bad mood rubbed off on her, causing her to cry? But somehow he sensed that he had nothing to do with her tears. It was as if she were no longer there, as if her inner self had flown away on the tide of music.

A light rain fell softly outside Frances's bedroom window, lulling her to sleep.

> Frances is floating on a calm turquoise sea, looking up at white bulging clouds. Music penetrates her ears, even though they are below the surface of the water. It is the 2nd movement from the Tchaikovsky *Concerto for Violin & Orchestra*. She closes her eyes to listen as the water supports her body in gentle undulating pulsations. She drifts in the sparkling swells, the water cool around her body; pin-points of light reflect upon her closed eyelids.
>
> She opens her eyes lazily to discover a hand above her holding a violin bow. The bow strokes her body, which she knows is the instrument. She is aroused and gives herself up to the bow, knowing that it is Adam. The music lifts her from the water towards the clouds. She is drifting in a sensual breeze, still being stroked by the bow, moving her body with the sound of the violin. Slowly she drifts into the clouds where she is surrounded by music and touch.
>
> Gradually the stroking of the bow becomes less pleasurable. It becomes harder and harder and the music changes to the sound of leaves battered and ripped by strong winds and rain. The stroking is now painful as the bow changes into the shape of hands coming around from behind her. They pull her down, down, down, until she hits the hard ground. She is looking up at a tree's canopy; it comes closer and closer to her face—suffocating, brutal. She screams as she tries to break free.

Frances sat upright amongst a tangle of sheets and cover. The echo of her scream faded into the walls. *Another dream*, she tried to tell herself sternly. *Just a dream.* Her eyes darted around the room looking for anything that might pose a threat in the shadows. She wiped at her face that was damp with perspiration and discovered the roots of her hair were also wet. She felt bruised, aching, as her gasping breaths rasped in her parched mouth. Plato suddenly jumped up onto the bed and nuzzled up against the shape of her body, his dark form in contrast to the pale cover. The contact calmed her and her breathing slowed. The curtains swayed in sinuous shadows, teased by a soft silent breeze that cooled her skin. Goose bumps crept over it and she snuggled back down underneath the cover. Somewhere below her a car swished past on a rain-wet road. It was a comforting sound of normality. The purring vibrated beside her as the cat settled down to sleep, its claws working into the cover. Frances gently pried Plato's claws from the thick white cotton, cushioning his paws in her hands.

"Hey. You shouldn't even be up here," she said softly. "So don't push it by punching holes in the bedclothes."

Plato looked at her with wide radiant eyes.

"Don't look at me like that. You know I'm an old softy."

She settled back down on the bed trying to will herself to sleep, although at the same time afraid that she might return to the same nightmare.

The first glimmerings of light filtered through the curtains into Frances's bedroom. She noticed the mounting traffic noises that grew with the light, as if drawn into the city upon the sun's rays. It had been a long night.

"Glad someone here can sleep," she whispered.

Plato woke suddenly with a soft light rumbling in his throat. His head turned back to watch her.

"Sorry," she said. "Didn't mean to disturb you."

He sat up and yawned expansively, his front paws stretching out in front of him.

"Breakfast?"

She padded out to the kitchen and leaned against the kitchen bench waiting for the kettle to boil. Plato's tongue darted quickly in and out of his water bowl, making soft quick lapping noises that were eventually drowned out by the kettle's rising clamour.

The morning air was fresh and clean after the night's rain. She could smell the eucalypts and pines in the Fitzroy Gardens as she sat on a chair on the balcony. It wouldn't be long before traffic fumes would mar the atmosphere, she knew; the time she had to enjoy her coffee outside was precious to her.

Memories of the nightmare cascaded through her mind in shifting fragments. Again she tried to piece them together, to make sense of them, to understand what had caused the trauma in her mind. She wondered why she had dreamed of Adam again, denying her germinating interest in him. A thousand excuses sprang to mind: her love of music, her love of the violin, her love of Tchaikovsky's music, the fact that Adam was a new person in her and Samuel's life. Then she remembered how her body had responded to the stroking bow in her dream and she felt ashamed, embarrassed. She felt dirty thinking that her body had betrayed her in the unconscious world.

Below, the treetops swayed in the light breeze, mesmerizing her. She watched them from tired, bloodshot eyes. Her face was drawn as she put her coffee mug down on the table. Nausea rose in her throat and she gulped rapidly before bursting into tears.

The morning's work had been uncommonly quiet with few customers and little conversation between Frances and Samuel. They went about their tasks automatically, only speaking when necessary, but without animosity. For some hours Samuel buried his head in the accounts while Frances sorted books as she took them out of boxes that had been delivered. From time to time Samuel's eyes followed her when she was unaware. He noticed the tired eyes, pale skin, trembling hands. *She's been working too hard. After all, she hasn't had a holiday since we became partners.*

She spent some moments in the back room and emerged with a coffee for both of them.

"Thanks," he said, putting his pen down to accept the mug. He hesitated. "You look terrible."

Her look was surprised and then, as if it had just occurred to her, "I'm having nightmares," she said simply.

"What are they about?"

"I...don't know. I can't remember."

"Is there anything I can...?"

"No. I'll be all right." She looked into her mug, hiding her expression.

"Why don't you go home?" Samuel walked around the other side of the counter to put his arm around her. "Have a rest."

"No..."

"We're not busy. I can cope with this crowd." He indicated the empty shop with a rueful smile.

"No." She shook her head. "I'd rather do the stocktake. Take my mind off it."

"Well, if you're sure..."

"Yes, I'm sure." She turned away from him. "We could make a start now."

The mask had dropped over her face, making it impossible for him to read it, and her body movements were the usual quick, definite signs of a no-nonsense purpose. It was obvious to him that she was avoiding the subject, but he shrugged as he respected her right to silence.

They worked on steadily for some time until Frances lost her place.

"The fourth page," he said. "Half-way down."

"Where?"

"There," he pointed at his own sheet. "Under science fiction."

At her blank look, he leaned over to point at the place on her own sheet, knocking the contents of her coffee mug over the stock list and some books.

"Oh, no!" Frances jumped up in alarm.

"Shit!"

"How clumsy!" She pulled a wad of tissues from a nearby box and mopped at the spilled coffee.

"I didn't mean to," he said petulantly.

"Oh, no! It's on these books too!" The spill had gone further than they'd thought and they quickly shifted everything away. "How could you?"

"It was an accident, for Christ's sake," he almost shouted.

"A stupid accident."

"I suppose you never have any."

"At least I'm careful."

"We can't all be perfect like you, can we?"

"I never said I was perfect."

"You act like it."

Tears gathered in her eyes and she sighed, "Oh, why are we arguing?"

Samuel indicated the mess they were mopping up. "Because of this." He opened another box of tissues and grabbed a wad. "Because you're tired."

"So it's my fault!" she said indignantly, her tears drying as suddenly as they had appeared.

"Well, you're not exactly yourself today."

"I'm sorry you find me so difficult to put up with," she replied haughtily, throwing a dripping handful of tissues into a rubbish bin. "Perhaps I'd better leave you in peace."

She marched out to the back room, then came straight out again with her handbag, and stalked out of the shop without looking back. Samuel's mouth gaped stupidly in surprise as he watched her cross the road and disappear out of sight. A wet trickle ran along his arm, staining his shirt sleeve.

"Shit!" He threw the wet tissues into the bin and hurried to change his shirt in the back room where he kept spares just in case.

Frances walked aimlessly through the gardens while she calmed down until she found herself in the leafy confines of the lower lake. She sat on a bench seat and watched the play of water as it spurted from the mouth of a turtle upon which sat a small bronze boy. His reflection rippled in the still waters of the lake and disappeared between the reeds. The chorus of the bird life and the pit-a-pat of the fountain smoothed away her self-righteous anger. She felt ashamed of her outburst. *Of course he didn't mean it*, she chided herself. *Accidents happen to anyone.* A pair of sparrows bathed in the lake, splashing enthusiastically, their heads dipping into the water from time to time. *I was horrible to him. He didn't deserve that.* The sun caught the beads of water as they shot up around the birds, making the droplets shine like crystalline jewels. *I'll apologise.* She yawned wearily. Her body felt like lead. It craved rest. *I'll have forty winks first.*

The path back to her apartment led past a row of fig trees. She stopped in front of them, searching the largest with her eyes. The twisted roots appeared like giant ribbons sculpted from the earth itself. They contorted in frozen postures that might have once held life, moved, rippled sinuously without warning. Fascinated, she edged inside one of the openings between the roots, then entered another and another, running her hands along the root walls.

Fear and nausea rose unbidden. Her heart raced in panic and she stood frozen, ensnared, in the confines of the opening. A wailing surged from somewhere near, increasing in volume until suddenly shut off by the appearance of startled joggers who passed the tree.

"Are you all right?" one of them asked, reaching towards her.

Embarrassed, Frances stumbled away from the tree, as if pushed by unseen hands. She realised the wailing had come from her. Running blindly, she blundered around the other side of the next tree, and leaned against its roots, crying silently, hoping the joggers would leave her alone. They resumed their run along the path away from her, the sound of their footsteps receding. Snatches of giggles mortified Frances as she realised they were laughing at her. She saw their heads turned back towards her and she shrank closer to the roots trying to disappear. Suddenly, a feeling of hands reaching out from the tree roots had her recoil in alarm from the tree.

"Who's there?" she cried.

Terrified, she backed away, expecting someone to come out from the other side of the tree. But no one appeared. No one threatened. She was alone.

The mask descended like slowly-dripping wax, covering each feature of her face until the fear was camouflaged and composure patterned her facade. She turned and walked slowly, heavily, towards her apartment without looking back.

Chapter 14

The doorbell shattered the quiet of Frances's apartment startling her and Plato as they lay on the sofa. She glanced in the hall mirror at her reflection that was a mess of mascara and red-rimmed eyes.

"Hello?" she said tentatively to the intercom.

"Frances? It's me…Adam."

She stared at the speaker in alarm.

"Hello?" His voice sounded metallic, without its usual deep melodious quality. "Are you there?"

"Oh, yes," she whispered.

"I took a chance, in case you were home, to return your book."

She looked in the mirror again and wiped at the mascara marks. They smudged across her cheeks; she licked her finger and tried again, unsuccessfully.

"Look, Samuel said you're unwell, so if you'd rather I come back another time…"

"No," she managed to say. "Come up."

The sound of the buzzer came through the speaker and she heard the door click behind Adam as he entered the building. She raced into the bathroom and splashed her face with cold water but her reflection told her she wasn't about to fool anyone. An eye drop in each eye and rapid blinking failed to brighten the whites. *Deep breath. Deep breath.* The mask refused to appear no matter how hard she willed it to. *Hell!* Panic caught her and she suddenly burst into tears. Horrified, she cried into the basin, splashing at her face furiously, her hair dripping with water.

He was at the door. His knock was hesitant at first. He waited, then tried again, more loudly this time. She looked up at the mirror. *Go on,* she told herself. *You can't leave him out there all day.*

She opened the door slowly, flicking her hair back and wiping at her eyes.

Adam looked at her with surprise. "I'm sorry. Did I interrupt you…?"

"No. No. It's all right." She stepped back for him to enter. "Come in."

He stood awkwardly in the small entrance, holding onto the Paganini book until she took it from him and placed it on a hall table.

"Thank you," he said simply.

She bit her lip and nodded, not trusting herself to speak. Her chin wobbled and she cupped it in her hand in an effort to disguise it.

"Frances?" His voice was a murmur as he dipped his head to look in her eyes.

She closed them but they betrayed her by leaking tears from under the lids. They trickled slowly down her cheeks. He dabbed at them gently with a handkerchief. As he moved closer, she caught a whiff of aftershave, and she opened her eyes to see him looking at her with concern.

"Do you want to talk about it?"

She shrugged.

"Well, can I get you a coffee…or something stronger?"

"I'm okay," she lied. "I'll make a coffee."

"Sure." The corners of his mouth turned up very slightly. "Can I help?"

Adam followed her into the kitchen and made small talk while she busied herself with the brewing of the coffee. The familiar task should have helped to calm her, but she was acutely aware of being alone with him. Her replies were awkward, short, contributing little to the conversation until they sat down at the table with their mugs.

After a momentary silence she spoke. "Samuel and I had an argument. It was all my fault." Adam waited until she was ready to continue. "I've been having nightmares. I don't understand them. I'm…tired I guess."

While they drank their coffee, she found herself opening up to Adam who proved to be a sympathetic listener. She told him of the argument, how she'd left *The Bookcase* in a huff, how her lack of sleep had caused her tearfulness, but she avoided the subject of her nightmares.

She finished by saying, "I'm sorry. You just caught me at a bad time. I'm not normally like this."

"I'm glad I *did* come. You need someone with you at a time like this."

A weak smile crept to her lips. "I'm all right. Really."

"Look—don't take this the wrong way, but don't you think you should seek some professional help?"

"I was horrible to Samuel."

"He would know you didn't mean it. You're not yourself."

"I feel terrible about it."

"I could take you."

She looked at him in surprise. "Where?"

"To see a counsellor or a…"

She shook her head. "I can deal with it myself."

"But, Frances, from what you say, you're not."

"No. I'll work it out." She jumped as the doorbell sounded. "It's probably Samuel."

As Frances disappeared from the kitchen, Adam sipped at the remains of his coffee. He heard her speak into the intercom and wait for Samuel to reach her front door. He swallowed the last mouthful, rinsed both mugs at the sink, and then followed Frances to the entry hall in time to see Samuel and Frances hugging warmly. Samuel looked over Frances's shoulder startled to see Adam standing there, then his expression changed to one of challenge. The two men stared at each other warily without speaking until Frances broke away from Samuel's over-long embrace. There was an awkward moment as Adam stood in the crowded entry hall waiting to get past them. Frances stepped back while Samuel remained with his arm now draped possessively around her shoulder.

Adam cleared his throat. "I'd better be off."

"You're not staying?" Frances shook off Samuel's arm.

"No," Adam shook his head. "I've got rehearsal. It's getting late."

"Thanks for calling in," she said simply, afraid to look into his eyes.

The silence between Samuel and Frances was palpable and she was unsure how to break it. They moved into the lounge room when Adam left, and she began to pace the room, stopping occasionally to look out of the french doors.

"A drink?" she offered.

"Okay."

She held up a bottle of Johnnie Walker.

"Thanks," he nodded.

She poured a generous measure for Samuel then went into the kitchen to add some ice to his glass, doing the same for herself, but adding brandy to her glass instead. He took the glass from her wordlessly and she resumed her pacing.

"Will you sit down?" he frowned. "You're making me dizzy!"

"I'm sorry," she said, stopping in her tracks, looking at him seated on the sofa. "About everything."

"You're tired," he said dismissively.

"That's no excuse." She sat beside him, a suspicion of tears in her eyes. "I've been horrible to you. I don't know why you put up with me."

"Neither do I," he laughed. "Because I love you dearly, I suppose." He looked at her closely, and squeezed her hand. "You need a break. You look terrible."

"Thank you so much."

"You're welcome." He paused. "Are you well enough to go out tonight?"

"I don't know."

"I think you should be in bed—resting."

"What about the tickets?"

"They're the least of my worries."

"It's too late to change them, though."

"Don't worry. I can still go."

"Perhaps you're right."

"That's my girl."

"I'm sorry."

He put his arm around her and gave her an affectionate hug. The familiar closeness between them had been re-established and they both felt relieved.

During the first half of the programme, Adam repeatedly tried to catch Samuel's eye who made a concerted effort to avoid Adam's gaze. The empty seat beside him seemed to gape hugely in the packed hall. He felt the cold space at his elbow. He missed Frances's company, her nearness, the enjoyment of sharing a performance together. It was the first time she had failed to be with him since the beginning of their partnership.

Samuel stood with his back to a wall, holding the programme in one hand and his champagne flute with the other. He wished Frances was with him to discuss the performance. To enjoy the champagne. To enjoy the familiarity of her companionship as they gazed at the crowd in the foyer. Sometimes he would remark upon the appearance of someone—perhaps in a derogatory sense—and she would frown at him. He liked that about her—the fact that she accepted everyone at face value and would refuse to criticize another's appearance. There was always something positive about her comments and she would defend the most slovenly appearance with sometimes the most ridiculous statement and they would both end up laughing. He was worried about her, not only from a selfish viewpoint, but from a genuine liking—loving—of her character, the person she was—his friend. He suspected a fragility in her psyche that threatened to smash her, and he had no idea how to prevent it or how to remedy it if it did happen.

"Frances not here?" Adam's voice broke into Samuel's thoughts.

"No."

"So I noticed." He waited for a response but when none came: "Is she all right?"

"No, she's not."

"Headache?"

"No."

"I'll call her…"

"I don't think so."

"Why not?"

"Look," Samuel drained his glass. "I think you'd better back off."

"What do you mean?" Adam's eyes were hard.

"You're coming on too strong…you're upsetting her."

"She hasn't said…"

"She wouldn't." Samuel looked into his empty glass, then met Adam's stare. "You're interfering in our life together…she was happy until you came along."

"She's given me no indication that…"

"You're putting her under pressure."

"And just how am I doing that?"

"I *know* her. I have done for many years." Samuel's look was triumphant. "We've a close bond and, I'm telling you now, I have no scruples about stopping you from coming between us."

Adam spoke carefully. "Are you telling me that you and Frances are in an intimate relationship?"

Samuel's hesitation was momentary. "Well, yes. Yes, we are."

"She didn't give me that impression."

"She doesn't owe you any explanations," he said angrily.

"I know that."

"So stop tormenting her."

"Are you sure it's me who's doing the tormenting?"

"I should know."

"Yes, I suppose you would," Adam said slowly.

"I'm telling you…for her sake."

"Hers—or yours?"

"What do you mean by that?"

The two men faced each other, oblivious of the crowd around them. A few bystanders leaned closer, fascinated by the verbal sparring between the concertmaster and the older man.

"I wonder who you really are thinking of."

"It's none of your business."

"Well, Frances can tell me that." He made as if to leave. "I'll ask her now."

Samuel grabbed him by the arm.

"I've asked her to marry me."

Adam was stunned as he shook off Samuel's hand. "You've what?"

His voice was loud over the din of conversation on every side. There was a momentary hush and curious faces waited for what would happen next. Adam and Samuel hunched closer, their faces turned towards the paintings that lined the wall.

"I asked her," Samuel answered in an exaggerated whisper.

"What did she say?"

"What do you think?"

"Well?"

"After all the years we've been together?"

"So?"

"My parents love her."

"Samuel…" he said impatiently, "did she accept?"

There was a momentary hesitation. "Of course she did."

"Oh."

"Yes."

"I had no idea…"

"You wouldn't."

"I didn't realise."

"Just so's you know. That's the situation."

Adam looked down at the floor, tracing a pattern on the carpet with his highly-polished shoe. He could see a distorted vision of Samuel reflected on the toe. The silence between them gave him time to sort through his mind the import of what Samuel had said, though he was doubtful of believing him.

"Yes, well, as you say," he said finally. "I'll keep my distance."

"I'd be grateful if you did."

The bell sounded as they looked at each other, any pretence of friendship dropped.

Samuel nodded as Adam turned on his heel and dissolved into the crowd. He wondered for a fleeting moment if he'd gone too far, then he shrugged it off, thinking with no small measure of satisfaction that Adam would be out of their lives and wouldn't discover his act of deception.

Chapter 15

Adam returned backstage a despondent man. *Why shouldn't she accept him?* He walked out onto the stage and tuned the orchestra. *Women! Better off without them.* The conductor waited for silence, baton raised. *I could have sworn Samuel was a...* The baton came down and the symphony began.

Samuel sat in his seat with a triumphant smile playing around his mouth. He leaned back confidently, his left arm draped proprietarily over the empty seat at his side as if she were really there. His right leg crossed the left one and it swayed slightly with the music, as if he had not a care in the world. His handsome features looked softer now, the creases smoothed out from his forehead, the severity of his expression relaxed. Now he was ready to meet Adam's gaze, but Adam concentrated on the crotchets and quavers scattered across the score on the music stand in front of him.

The concert over, Adam left the stage deep in thought, hardly aware of his surroundings.

"See you soon." The voice broke into his thoughts.

"What?" He looked in the direction of the voice. "Oh," he said to himself, as he realised the voice belonged to that of a harpist as she looked down at her mobile phone.

He stopped, staring at the mobile, then began to walk up and down fiddling with his own in his pocket. *Probably too late.* His watch showed ten thirty-five. *Don't want to wake her.* He walked into the men's toilet, hesitated and then returned out to the corridor. He took out his mobile, weighing it in his hand, then dropped it back into his pocket, thumping the nearest wall. A few other musicians called out to him and he waved back, then made as if to walk away. *I don't believe him, damn it!* It was now ten thirty-eight. Her number rang once.

"Hello?"

"Frances," he began without any preliminaries. "I was concerned when I saw your seat was vacant."

There was a slight pause before she responded. "I'm just not feeling the best tonight."

"Samuel told me."

"Oh? You saw him?"

"Yes."

"Where are you now?"

"Backstage."

"How was the concert?"

"Fine. I'm sorry you missed it."

"Me too."

"Did I wake you?"

"No."

He waited for a moment, then continued. "Are you very ill?"

"Not really. Just a little tired."

"Frances." He leaned his back against the wall and took a deep breath. "I'm sorry if I've been upsetting you. And …congratulations."

"What do you mean?"

"Samuel…ah…told me. About your…ah…marriage plans."

"What?" Her tone was incredulous.

He rushed on. "So I'll understand if you'd rather not see me."

There was a momentary pause. "What did he say?"

"That he's asked you to marry him."

He thought he heard her smother a giggle.

"Yes he did," she said in a strained voice, "but …"

"And I didn't realise."

She refrained from answering and he paused to wait for her reply. Eventually he said, "I'm sorry if I was making a nuisance of myself."

"Adam, listen." Her voice shook. Adam wasn't sure if she was about to cry or laugh. "Samuel did ask me to marry him, but I said no."

He looked at his mobile in surprise. "Pardon?"

"I said no."

"You did?"

"Yes."

"But he told me..."

"Poor old Samuel."

"Then you're not getting married?"

She burst out laughing. "No, I'm not." And she continued to giggle without restraint.

"Well, that's a relief!"

The giggling stopped suddenly.

"Frances? Are you there?"

"Yes."

"Have I been butting in?"

"No. We enjoy your company."

"Samuel doesn't."

"Oh, he's a silly old thing sometimes. He doesn't mean anything by it."

"So..." he said carefully, "we're still friends?"

"Of course," she replied warmly. "If you want to be."

He looked up at the ceiling in relief, smiling hugely, and mouthed the words *thank you.* "Very much," he replied.

"Then that's settled." There was reassurance in her voice.

He smiled into the phone. "Are you sleepy?"

"Not really."

"I can be at your place..." he consulted his watch, "no later than eleven."

"What do you mean?"

"I'm coming over to see you."

"Tonight?" Her voice was a croak.

"Yes."

"You'll be tired."

"It takes me ages to wind down after a concert."

"Adam?" There was a pause. "Why are you coming?"

"Because I missed you tonight," he said sincerely. "Your seat looked very empty—lonely."

"Oh?"

"I'll see you around eleven."

Adam disconnected before she had a chance to object. He had a huge grin on his face.

Frances kept the mobile to her ear until the line went dead. Her heart raced as she put the mobile on her bedside table. She clutched her neck, her thoughts in a frantic jumble. *He's coming! Here! Now!* Her dressing gown gaped at the neck and she looked down at it in horror. She jumped up quickly and hurried into her bedroom, pulling out a pair of slacks and a loose top. The reflection in the mirror worried her and she spent some anxious moments in the bathroom trying to conjure up a relaxed facade with the aid of concealer under her eyes and a soft lipstick.

By the time he arrived she was sitting on the sofa with Plato trying to calm her jitters. Mozart played softly in the background as she re-read the first page of a book for the fifth time. Both she and Plato jumped when the door bell sounded.

When she opened the door, she took Adam's violin case from him and placed it carefully on the hall table. He handed her a single gardenia. She took it from him, aware of the blush that crept into her face, and sniffed at its perfume appreciatively as she led the way into the lounge room.

He passed her a bottle of sleeping pills as they sat opposite each other in the lounge room.

Frances turned the bottle over in her hand, reading the label. "Where did you get them at this hour?"

"An all night chemist."

"Oh?"

"Mum swears by them," he said. "They're herbal."

"Does she have much trouble sleeping?"

"Only when she's worried about one of us," he smiled. "You know what big families are like."

"No, I don't." She held the gardenia up to her nose again.

He watched her for a moment. "No brothers or sisters?"

"No."

"Your parents—do you see much of them?"

"Would you like a cup of tea?" Her tone was suddenly brittle.

The abrupt change of tack surprised him. He looked at her enquiringly, but she failed to continue. Without warning she rose from her chair and disappeared into the kitchen. The sound of running water and the clatter of crockery met his ears. He decided to join her, along with Plato who walked in front of him, tail raised in what resembled a question mark. He thought how similar Plato was to his mother's cat who had an annoying habit of always walking in front of him and tripping him up. He placed his feet carefully so as not to step on the cat, and waited for the black-coated Plato to insinuate himself around the corner of the kitchen door. He bent down and stroked the shining fur along the curve of the spine. It quivered sensually from the base of the neck right along to the tip of the tail. Plato turned his emerald eyes up to Adam, expecting more of the same. Adam tickled him behind an ear then straightened to see Frances working at a furious pace making tea.

He had time to observe her while her back was turned. Her usual calm, controlled demeanour was replaced by jerky, frantic movements. Her back was stiff, her body seemingly coiled tightly. Not for the first time, Adam wondered at her unpredictable behaviour and whether she would confide in him again.

"So it's those nightmares keeping you awake at nights?" he asked casually as he walked into the kitchen.

"Yes," she whispered finally into the teapot.

"What're they about?"

She hesitated a moment before replying. "Mostly trees." Reaching into an overhead cupboard she searched amongst a variety of packets of tea before adding, "Huge trees."

"What happens?"

"Earl Grey okay?"

"Fine. What happens with the trees?"

Her hands stopped on the packet as she paused. "There are big roots that twist up and around me," she whispered. "There are hands—they grab me." Her voice rose quickly. "Brutal hands. Storms." He could sense alarm in her voice.

He spoke carefully. "Who do the hands belong to?"

"Would you like biscuits and cheese?" Her manner was suddenly over-bright—forced. Plato rubbed against her legs and she absently leaned down to pat him before opening another cupboard door. "Or sweet biscuits?" She dragged plastic containers and tins out of the cupboards, banging them on the bench. "I think I've got some fruit cake here too." Whirling around, she pulled out a toaster. "Or, I can toast some raisin bread. I bought it yesterday from the bakery around the corner. It's a little heavy, but delicious." She opened the fridge and took out a carton. "Do you like milk in your tea? No? Black with a slice of lemon? I think I've got some lemons here in the fridge. Let me have a look. One of our customers brings them in. I haven't bought a lemon for a couple of years now. Such a nice lady she is too. She's a widow, you know. Reads such a lot of books…"

"What sort of tree?" he broke in, determined to swing her back to the subject but mindful of the danger that he might push her too far. He'd not seen her so flustered, so lacking in control—so raw.

"Oh, God," she said breathlessly. "I don't know…like them." Her fingers stabbed the air violently in the direction of the gardens.

"Out there?" His gaze followed her hand.

"Yes. The Morton Bay figs." Her eyes were wild as she looked in the direction of the gardens through the doorway. "They're weird."

"Because of the dreams?"

She dragged her gaze away from the doorway and turned abruptly to the kitchen bench. "Samuel gave me this tea pot, you know. Last Christmas I think it was. He bought it in a little shop in Hobart last time he was there. It keeps the tea hot. My other one didn't. If you wanted another cup, it was lukewarm by the time you poured it. I like my tea hot, don't you?"

Adam gently took the tea pot from her hands and placed it deliberately on the bench. His calm movements stilled her agitated fussing around the kitchen, and she sagged against the bench, head down, embarrassed by her absurd prattling.

"The dreams," he insisted. "How long have you had them?"

"Ever since I moved in here—no," she paused thinking, then continued slowly. "I used to have them when I was a child."

"But they started again here?"

She nodded. "I don't understand where they're coming from," she said to the floor. "Or what's happening to me. I feel depressed all the time…scared…and don't know why."

Her head raised slowly and he saw tears in her eyes. She looked at him in mute appeal. His breath stopped for several moments, imprisoned in his chest, as he fought the urge to close the small gap between them. His natural instinct was to put his arms around her, to hold her, but he was afraid that if he did, he risked breaking what closeness he had established. Instead, he handed her his handkerchief and turned to fill a glass from the tap, taking the few seconds to control his breathing.

The handkerchief remained folded, crushed in her hand as she watched him. Taking the offered glass of water, she took a sip, then choked on it, causing a coughing fit. She gasped, trying to catch her breath, and he rubbed at her back in an effort to stop the fit. As the coughing gradually subsided, and he continued to rub her back, he found his arms around her. She was unmoving as his arms tightened, drawing her into his chest. A faint whiff of perfume and the softness of her hair under his chin, along with the feel of her body next to his, set his pulse racing. Without thinking he bent to nuzzle into her neck. Startled, her head snapped up to face him, and they looked for a long moment into each other's eyes, neither of them moving. Adam wondered if she could hear his heart roaring. It surged under his rib cage, sending blood hurtling through every vein and artery. Nothing else existed but Frances in that moment. Reason, and his normal discretion, were lost as his head bent slowly to kiss her, his lips brushing hers with feather-soft tingling strokes, then with rising passion as the taste of salt on her lips dissolved into the softness of her mouth. For a fleeting moment she responded, then pushed him away from her.

"Don't!" she spat at him, wiping her mouth with the back of her hand. "I thought I could trust you."

"You can!"

"If I'd known you would…"

"Damn it, Frances," he said grimly, his jaw clenching. "You're a very attractive woman."

She backed away from him. "You've abused our friendship!"

"By showing you how I feel? It was only a kiss, for God's sake. Calm down."

"You come up here…" she said, wiping at her mouth again. "I let you in in good faith…"

"Okay. I overstepped the mark." He took a deep breath. "It won't happen again."

"You promise?"

"Yes, I promise."

She looked at him long and searchingly, making up her mind about whether she could trust him again. He turned to the sink, clenching his hands on its edge, looking out of the window as he regained his self-control. *Stupid!* The view of the flood-lit gardens was lost on him as he berated himself for frightening her. *But I'm only human…*

"Adam?"

He turned to face her and was surprised to see a tentative, though trembling, smile on her lips.

"Would you like that cup of tea now?"

With relief he smiled back at her, and held out his hands for the tray that she was holding.

"I'd love it," he replied.

Their cups were empty when Frances leaned over to pick up the bottle of sleeping pills from the coffee table in the lounge room. They had drunk their tea in silence.

"I'm terrified of going to sleep…and what I'll find there."

"Hopefully they'll give you a dreamless sleep," he said nodding in the direction of the pills. "Relax you."

"They'd have to be a wonder drug," she said doubtfully.

"Or I could play for you—let the music unwind you."

With that, he got up from his chair to retrieve his violin case from the hall table. Sitting down again, he opened the case and took out the violin. He heard her sudden intake of breath and looked up to see her face flushed with pleasure.

"How about a lullaby?" he asked softly as he took out the bow and stood in front of her.

She nodded, unable to speak lest she betray how thrilled and yet embarrassed she felt.

"Well, lie back against the cushions and forget about everything."

When she did as he suggested, he began to play the *Barcarole* from Offenbach's *Gaité Parisiennne*. With satisfaction he saw her eyes close as she allowed the music to calm her. It was a rare opportunity for him to observe her so closely as he played, sensitive to her every tiny movement. Her eyelids fluttered as her eyes moved under them, the tightness around her mouth and jaw lessened as her head relaxed into the cushions. The soft light from a nearby lamp reflected chestnut highlights in her dark hair as it fell away from her face. He remembered how soft and fragrant it was as it had brushed against his chin and he longed to touch it, feel it sweep across his bare chest. Aside from the hint of dark circles underneath her eyes, her skin was flawless—like the palest of porcelain.

He kneeled close to her as he continued, the notes soft in their persuasion of sleep, and he studied the lips that had, for the briefest of moments, responded to his own. As if sensing his scrutiny, her eyes opened slowly and, in a dreamlike state, she met his gaze. His hand guided the bow lightly across the strings as the last note died away. Eyes locked, they remained motionless, mute, tied by the music, frozen in the same positions— Frances reclined with half-open eyes regarding him, Adam still with the violin and bow held midair—until he broke the spell and slowly lowered the instrument. The silence in the room was deafening as he desperately tried to control the arousal of his body and mind.

"Look…" he managed to croak, "how about I stay here for the night? On the couch."

Frances's peaceful expression changed to a frown.

"I promise to behave," he assured her. "I'll just be out here if you need me."

"There's nothing you can do." Her face had tightened up.

"A shoulder to cry on?" He grinned ruefully. "It's tried and tested."

"Oh, I couldn't…"

"It's nearly dawn anyway! I have to come back for rehearsals in…" he said looking at his watch, "…five hours."

She felt guilty. "I've been such a wet blanket, haven't I? And you've got so far to travel!"

"Talking about blankets—have you got one?" He rose from his kneeling position and sat back on a chair. "And a spare toothbrush?"

"Oh, all right," she gave in. "It would be rotten of me to kick you out at this hour." She got up from the couch and looked down at it. "But the couch may not be very comfortable for you."

"I can sleep anywhere," he assured her.

She disappeared into her bedroom without another word and reappeared with a blanket and pillows in her arms. Throwing them onto the couch, she went into the bathroom and came out with a toothbrush and a towel.

"If you need me, I'm here," he said, taking them from her.

"I know."

"Sleep well."

"I hope so."

As she reached her bedroom door, she stopped and turned around, holding onto the door frame.

"Adam?"

"Umm…?"

"Thanks for everything."

"Anytime."

She hesitated. "I loved the *Barcarole*."

"Did it help?"

She nodded, then said softly, "Goodnight."

"'Night."

Frances regarded him for a moment and then went into her bedroom, closing the door behind her. He heard a key turn in the lock and he smiled to himself as he made his way to the bathroom.

On the other side of the door, Frances stood with her hand still clutching the key in the lock. She listened as he moved into the bathroom, heard a tap turn on, the running of water, the toilet flush, then held her breath as she sensed his return to the lounge room. There was a faint, unfamiliar click which she supposed to be the catch on his violin case. She pictured him placing it into its soft velvet cushioning, and sliding the bow into its place in the lid. Her heartbeats quickened as she remembered him kneeling in front of her, playing to her—only her. How perfectly each note was created to float in the air and be successively replaced by the next and the next and the next. How the subtle smell of rosin competed in her nostrils with the smell of him. How amazing such delicate notes and movements came from such a powerful body.

As she settled under the sheets, Plato jumped up on the bed and sat regarding her, his emerald eyes unblinking as they followed her every movement.

"I know," she told him quietly, "I'm an idiot."

Plato purred as she rubbed him behind the ears.

"I shouldn't have let him stay. I shouldn't have told him about the nightmares. I shouldn't have let him kiss me. I shouldn't have…"

Her words trailed off as her hand dropped onto the bed. A slight smile crept across her lips as, in the doorway to a beginning dream, the smell of rosin blended with the smell of a violinist and the taste of his lips dripped into her own as he drew her to him. They drifted into another realm where dreams make anything possible and reality blurs on the edges.

Adam had just fallen into a deep sleep when he was awakened by a piercing scream. It rose to a frightful note and then cut off abruptly to be replaced by muffled moaning and crying. Disturbed from his sleep, he was disoriented and fell off the couch in a tangle of blanket and pillows. Stumbling over furniture in the dark lounge room, his hands explored the walls, not knowing where the lights were. He followed the sounds to what he knew to be Frances's bedroom and tried the door. Finding it still locked, he knocked.

"Frances?"

The moaning continued.

"Frances?" He called louder this time, knocking loudly.

"Are you okay?"

Suddenly the moaning stopped and there was silence until a faint sobbing reached his ears through the closed door.

"Frances! Open the door!"

Finally he heard a faint click and the door opened slowly to reveal Frances leaning against the wall, crying into her hands. He pulled her gently into the lounge room and led her across to the couch where they both sat down together.

"Pretty bad, eh?" he asked, mopping at her tears with his handkerchief. "The trees?"

"Oh, Adam," she cried. "It was so horrible. I think I'm going mad."

"Can you remember it?"

"The hands…rain…lightning…trees."

"Does it make any sense to you?"

"No," she shook her head. "None of it."

"We'll just stay here then. Together. If you have another nightmare, I'll be here with you."

His arms went around her and she cried into his chest until her sobs finally subsided.

"Adam?" Her voice was muffled.

"Umm?"

"You won't leave?"

"Not a chance."

He leaned back against the cushions and pillows, taking her with him. She went without protest, her body gradually relaxing as she fell into a deep sleep, protected by Adam's warmth and strong body. He gently brushed her sweat-soaked hair away from her forehead, his hand hesitating mid-air as Plato landed soundlessly on the arm of the couch. The emerald eyes regarded him unblinkingly, then turned their gaze to Frances. Adam watched the cat as it studied the sleeping woman for a long moment, until the movement of Adam's hand resumed its slow stroking of Frances's hair, and he found himself the object of Plato's gaze again. *Don't move*, he willed it. *Leave her in peace.* A low rumbling purr began as Plato's body relaxed onto the wide couch arm. Adam saw the claws dig into the upholstery, the emerald green eyes half-closing. *Good cat!*

Afraid to move in case he woke her, Adam lay with her in his arms, eyes wide open as he waited out the night, happy to be just where he was.

Chapter 16

Adam moved his neck from side to side as he sat opposite Frances at the kitchen table. The hours of lying in the same position had taken their toll upon his neck and back muscles and he craved a long hot shower to loosen them up.

But he would have stayed there, holding her, for as long as it took for her to have a peaceful sleep. And that's what she did have while she had remained curled up against him. The embarrassment of waking in his arms, the intimacy of their position together on the couch, had caused her to jump up quickly and make a hasty retreat to the bathroom. She had wondered if he'd seen the blush that had swamped her face and neck.

"Not hungry?" he asked, as she pushed the contents of her plate around.

She shook her head, staring into the plate. The scrambled eggs had sat long enough on the toast to make it soggy, Adam noticed. He thought how exhausted she looked—almost haggard. *I must look pretty haggard myself*, he thought, feeling the roughness of the night's growth on his face.

"Have you seen anyone about this—ever?"

"No."

"You don't want to?"

"No."

"Why?"

"I'm afraid." She paused as she looked up at him over the table. "I know I should—but I can't."

"Why do you cry during concerts?" he asked suddenly.

"Pardon?" She looked at him, startled.

The sudden ring of the phone made her jump, but she remained where she was, staring at him in puzzlement.

"Would you like me to answer it?"

She shrugged.

"Hello?" She watched him as he listened into the ear piece. "Yes, it's Adam." He listened again. "No—she had a bad night." His eyes met hers. "Yes—I was here…" His jaw tightened. "I don't know…I'll ask her."

Adam put the receiver down and sat opposite Frances, taking her hands in his. "It's Samuel. He wants to know if you're going in today."

"I'll talk to him," she said finally as she got up slowly, taking her hands away.

"Hello, Samuel." She paused, listening. "Oh, I'm fine…I'd prefer to go in. Rather be busy…No. No. I'll walk across…Yes—fresh air." She frowned. "Stop worrying. I'll be fine…Yes. See you soon."

She put the receiver back deliberately and turned to the table to find Adam smiling at her. Confusion flustered her and she switched her attention to Plato who had finished eating his breakfast and was rubbing up against her leg.

"Yes," she said, picking him up. "You'll have to do without me today." As she stroked him, she said to Adam, "I'd better get ready for work."

"You're going in?"

"Yes, he needs me."

As soon as Frances arrived at *The Bookcase*, she was swept up in a chaotic morning in which *Poet's Corner* overflowed with university students where Samuel was holding court, as well as a steady stream of customers to attend to. She was thankful that she had no time to dwell upon the previous night's events, though she'd had the opportunity to mull over it on the way to work.

Her feelings were mixed in a jumble of emotions: consternation, anger, yet amusement at Samuel's deliberate lie to Adam;

anger at Adam's taken liberty of kissing her when she was at her most vulnerable—yet gratitude for his support and comfort during the night. She'd touched her lips unconsciously as she walked through the gardens, catching herself reliving his kiss; they tingled at the memory. The smell of him as she'd curled up against him, the feel of his solid body through his shirt, made her blush as she remembered.

"Good night, was it?" Samuel hissed in her ear as he passed her on his way to get a reference book from a shelf near where Frances was standing.

"Pardon?"

"It must have been some night—rhapsodic." Samuel pretended he was looking through one of the books, his back to *Poet's Corner*.

"What are you talking about?"

He looked at her sideways and whispered, "Did he play his violin for you before the big moment?"

"How dare you!" She blushed at his closeness to the truth. "You don't know what you're talking about."

"No? I wasn't aware you had male tenants. Or have I been missing something? Trouble is, all that TLC's wearing you out."

"Hey, Samuel!" someone called out. "You got the article?"

"Coming," he called back. "Just trying to cross reference it."

"If you're insinuating that…"

"No need to insinuate, dear girl. It's obvious. Making up for lost time, are you?"

"Samuel, I don't owe you any explanation as to what goes on in my apartment. But, I'll tell you this…" she said, her voice rising with the noise level increasing in *Poet's Corner*, drowning out her words to possible listeners. "I've not had a decent night's sleep for…weeks…months. I'm suffering extremely terrifying nightmares that are leaving me exhausted—desperate. I don't know how much more of this I can take! And a passionate love affair is the last thing on my mind. Do I make myself clear?"

Horrified, Samuel realised how wrong he'd been. He took her hands in his, searching her face with concern in his eyes.

"You look ghastly," he said at last.

"Thanks a lot."

"You know what I mean."

"Yes, I know."

"You can't go on like this." He pulled a business card out of his wallet, offering it to her. "I've got the name of a good psychiatrist—a friend of mine."

"He doesn't seem to be helping you much," she flared at him, brushing his hand away.

"What...?"

"For pathological mendacity?" Her voice dripped sarcasm.

"Pardon?"

"Lying."

"Oh."

There was an uncomfortable silence as their eyes met—his wary and ashamed, hers blazing.

"Samuel!" The clamour was more insistent. "Hey, we're losing the argument here."

"Be right there," Samuel called over the din.

Frances took a number of books from the shelf, her mouth tight, brooking no argument. Samuel looked from her to the students and back again, torn between his desire to talk more with her and his duty to his customers.

"Go on," she pushed him towards them.

"How about going up to Mother's on the weekend?" he asked suddenly.

"What?"

"Change of scenery?"

"Yes," she conceded, despite herself. "We need to talk. About Adam."

He looked at her warily. "All right. We'll get Mandy in to do Saturday."

"What? Leave tomorrow night?"

"Yes. That'll give you two full days out."

"That'd be lovely."

As he turned to join the students in *Poet's Corner* he caught a glimpse of a deliberate change creep across her face. It wiped the expression of fury and surprise from her mouth and eyes and he imagined the trickle of sarcasm dissolving in her throat. It was at times like these that she almost frightened him, he thought.

Samuel held the car door open for Frances as she stepped into the front seat. He closed the door and walked around the car, checking the boot as he went.

"Now you've got everything?" he asked as he turned the key in the ignition.

"Yes," she replied, looking behind. "You put the flowers for your mother in the boot?"

He nodded. "You left the food out for Plato?"

"I did," she smiled.

"Okay, let's away!"

They both wore the mask of friendship but the strain in their voices belied the lightness of their conversation.

He pulled out into the traffic as Frances's phone began to ring on her desk in the lounge room. Plato jumped up onto the desk, scattering some papers onto the floor. He looked at the phone, waiting for the answering machine to pick up the call. He liked to listen to Frances's voice when it started, even though his level of understanding failed to enlighten him how she could be inside the machine. Usually there would be another voice after hers. He pawed at the machine, but it didn't start up. Frances had forgotten to switch it on. The phone continued to ring for some time and then stopped abruptly.

Adam waited until Frances's phone rang out. An hour later, he held the phone to his ear again, then hung up after getting no response. He then tried her mobile. The voice message he received was transmitted from inside the handbag she'd swapped that morning.

Plato was woken again by the phone's insistent ringing. He yawned and stretched across the desk, then decided to go and find something to eat. He padded into the kitchen and buried his head in a large bowl filled to the brim with dry food. He purred with pleasure, forgetting about the phone.

Adam jabbed at the end call button roughly. "I give up!"

By the time Samuel had driven out of the city traffic, the silence inside the car was absolute. For once even the radio was not switched on. Normally he and Frances would be engaged in energetic conversation that would last until their destination, only occasionally pausing to hum to a favourite passage of a concerto or symphony playing on the radio. This time, however, they were both busy with their thoughts, wondering how to start the subject that they had avoided until now. Twice Samuel opened his mouth to say something, even uttering the first syllable, but then covering the sound with a furtive cough.

"Did you really think you'd get away with it?" she asked, breaking the silence.

"I didn't think it through that far."

"Well why on earth did you…?"

"A knee-jerk reaction."

"To what?"

"His interference. His putting you under pressure. His assumption he had some right to…"

"He has no rights when it comes to me."

"Well, I didn't know that, did I," Samuel replied petulantly.

"But to tell him we were…"

"Getting married?"

"Yes."

Samuel laughed. "You should have seen his face."

"I hardly think it a laughing matter," she said stiffly.

"No. Not at all." He was immediately contrite, stealing a sideways glance at her as he drove along the brightly-lit highway. She was staring ahead, her profile appearing blurred in the soft light reflected from the dashboard. He pulled over to the side of the road and turned the engine off.

"Look," he said, taking her hand in his. "I'm sorry. I'm an idiot. I'm possessive, I'm jealous…all those things. I just can't stand the thought of losing you and my world slipping away."

"You…"

"No, let me finish," he told her. "When he thought you were sick, he was going to ring you. I thought he'd go to your place, win you over, make love to you, then whisk you away to some far exotic place and I'd never see you again."

Frances opened her mouth to speak but stopped as he squeezed her hand.

"I know it was irrational. It all raced through my mind in a split second and then he demanded to know if we were in some sort of intimate relationship. It…the lie…just happened. And when it did, it sounded right and I just let it go on."

He released her hand thumping the steering wheel in frustration. "I nearly believed it, you know. I felt triumphant—almost…normal. Just what my parents would want."

"Samuel."

"Yes?" He turned to look at her.

"Forget it."

"But…"

"It's not an issue anymore."

The weekend with Samuel's parents drifted past in a pleasant blur for Frances of home-cooked meals, games of Scrabble, relaxed conversation and time to read without the demands of work to distract her. She slept soundly and woke refreshed to take early-morning walks to the lake where she sat on the bridge and watched the mayhem of the local birds' existence. A birdcall suddenly reminded her of a violin playing *The Lark Ascending*. Her thoughts turned to Adam and she wondered if she should have told him that she was going away for the weekend. And then she asked herself why she should inform him of her whereabouts anyway, and that they were nothing to each other, and that he probably wouldn't care where she was. *Well, he might...*

Frances opened the door of her apartment and Samuel followed her in with her suitcase. He disappeared into her bedroom with it as she made a fuss of Plato.

"Did you miss me?" she asked as he purred from every muscle of his body. His emerald eyes regarded her seriously.

The phone rang as Samuel came out of the bedroom. "Will I get it?"

"Thanks," she said distractedly, as she continued to cuddle Plato.

He picked up the receiver. "Hello?" He frowned. "Who?"

Frances joined him in the lounge room to see who was calling. Samuel held out the phone to her as if it was contaminated.

"Hello?" She paused. "Oh, hello, Adam...yes, we've been away for the weekend...spur of the moment." She smiled. "Much better, thanks...next Saturday?" She put Plato down. "Yes, I think so. Let me check my diary."

She put the receiver down on the desk and flicked through her diary. Samuel watched her every move as she picked up the phone again.

"Yes, we do have seats for that one. You're playing? Oh, good." She looked out of the window as she listened. "Yes. See you then…bye."

As she put the phone down, she bent to retrieve the papers Plato had scattered.

"You've been up here again," she scolded him. "Naughty."

Samuel stood watching her expectantly. "That was sweet of Adam," she said.

"What was?"

"He rang to see if I was feeling better." She turned away from Samuel to hide the blush she could feel rising from her neck.

"Very sweet," he replied sarcastically.

At his tone, Frances spun around to look at him quizzically. She opened her mouth to say something but closed it again. *Nothing's changed,* she thought grimly as she felt her muscles become taut in defence.

Chapter 17

Frances fiddled with her glass while she pretended interest in the programme. She looked up now and again to see if Adam would appear, especially now that Samuel had gone to the toilet. Try as she might, it was difficult not to hope for Adam's appearance and that if he did appear, he would do so while Samuel was absent. At least they wouldn't have to put up with Samuel's scowling and sarcasm which made conversation so uncomfortable.

She asked herself why he couldn't accept the friendship with Adam. After all, there was no harm in it, was there? Samuel's jealousy was ridiculous. Hopefully their conversation in the car on the way to his parents' place had convinced him that he had nothing to fear from Adam's inclusion in their life. It was a purely platonic friendship with Adam—she'd insisted upon that—and Samuel would just have to accept it. She tried to push aside the memory of Adam's kiss and his apparent attraction to her. He'd just have to learn where he stood.

A voice broke into her musings.

"Penny for your thoughts?"

She looked up to see Adam standing right in front of her. It felt like the wind had been knocked out of her as his mouth broke into a smile.

Her own mouth curved into a corresponding smile. "Oh, nothing much."

He bent towards her. "The nightmares…still happening?"

Frances nodded, the smile leaving her eyes.

"You're looking a little less depressed, though," he was quick to say. "The weekend away must have done you good."

"I do feel better," she replied. "And thanks for the other night."

"Anytime."

Adam looked around the crowd and then back to Frances with a question in his eye which she failed to notice.

"You're a good friend," she continued.

"I hope so." He paused as he looked for any sight of Samuel again. "Frances?"

"Yes?"

"Would you come out to dinner with me?"

"Wait 'till Samuel comes and…"

"Not with Samuel," he said quietly, but firmly.

"Just me?" She looked surprised.

He nodded. "Just you."

"I don't know…I…"

"Please?"

"No Samuel?"

With a mock seriousness that belied the smile quivering at the corners of his mouth, he said, "No Samuel."

"Why?"

"Come on, Frances," he said, suddenly impatient. "You're not stupid!"

She blushed as she retorted, "No, I'm not."

"Well then?"

She regarded him steadily, thinking.

"Do I frighten you?" Before she had a chance to answer, he said carefully, "Or do you frighten yourself?"

"What *are* you talking about?"

Adam's mouth tightened into an angry line. "Food. Conversation. Getting to know each other. Is that so horrifying?"

He looked up to see Samuel approaching.

"Look, do you want to dine with me or not? Yes or no."

Her chin rose defiantly, then she looked over her shoulder quickly to see Samuel struggling through a tight-knit group of people. Despite herself, she nodded.

"All right, then," she said slowly, her eyes on Samuel. "Yes, I'll do it."

Samuel broke through the crowd and joined them, looking from one to the other suspiciously, especially as they both stood without speaking. Frances became suddenly busy with her drink, her downcast eyes hiding her expression. She suddenly felt alarmed at the thought of what she'd agreed to.

"Adam," Samuel began. "You've…"

He was interrupted by the bell ringing.

Adam turned to go. "Sorry, Samuel. Have to catch you another time."

The night had finally arrived, due to Adam's discreet persistence—the night that Frances had tried to put off a number of times with all manner of excuses.

Plato sat on the bathroom bench watching his mistress apply the finishing touches to her sparse make-up. She looked at herself in exasperation.

"Why did I get myself into this?"

She swivelled a lipstick out of its tube and traced the outline of her upper lip with a shaking hand.

"Oh, hell!"

The outline was crooked; she quickly wiped it clean and started again.

"Don't know why I'm bothering," she mumbled. "After all, I'm not trying to impress anyone."

Plato followed her reflection in the mirror, his green eyes large and unwavering. She stopped to look at him.

"I don't have to impress you, do I?" she crooned, tickling him under the chin.

Suddenly the doorbell rang.

Taking a step back, she regarded her handiwork.

"It'll have to do."

When Frances opened the door, Adam held out a gift-wrapped pot which contained an exotic flowering cactus. She took it from him, raising an eyebrow as she read the label.

"Unusual." She looked from the label to him. "Thank you…I think."

"For an unusual woman," he said quietly, with a smile playing around his eyes. "It reminds me of you."

"The spines?"

He nodded. "And the ability to bloom without water."

She laughed. "Nice compliment!"

"It needs nourishment, you know, despite its reputation. It needs love."

She looked at him quizzically.

"Can you do that?" he asked.

Plato rubbed against her legs and she put the plant on the hall table to pick him up, deliberately caressing him.

Her chin went up defiantly. "Yes, I can do that."

They stood regarding each other for a few moments in silence until Frances looked away.

"Where are we going?" she asked brightly.

"I've booked us into Parklands."

"Oh, good."

"How's your appetite?"

"Not ravenous."

"Let's jog through the park to work it up, then."

"In these heels?"

Adam looked down at her feet that were clad in black high-heeled sandals. They matched the simple black dress that was adorned with a short string of cultured pearls. She wore matching earrings, he noticed.

"Well, a sedate walk," he conceded.

"I'd like that."

Frances took a small evening bag from the hall table. Adam opened the door for her and they walked out to the lift together.

They stood looking at the indicator light as it changed from floor to floor. The tension between them was electric, neither speaking, both acutely aware of the other standing so close. At last the door opened and they entered the lift. A confusion of their reflections stared back at them from the mirrored walls. She saw him looking at her and she looked away to study the floor buttons. The door swished closed quietly and they dropped slowly, smoothly to the ground floor.

The mild late summer evening was full of the shrieks of birds returning to their nests after a busy day scavenging for food. Despite the surrounding city's traffic fumes and earlier chaos, on entering the gardens Frances and Adam seemed to enter a new, clean, quiet world. Suddenly they broke into conversation, the tension relaxing, and they fell into an easy walk along a concrete path that led through the neat green lawns and well-spaced trees.

So engrossed in what Adam was saying about the complexities of a musician's life, Frances failed to notice the row of Moreton Bay Fig trees that they were passing. He stopped suddenly.

"Fig trees!"

She stopped in her tracks, unease creeping over her.

"Do you mind stopping for a minute? I'd like to see them," he said, walking over to touch the twisted roots.

Without answering him, Frances abruptly strode away from the trees, taking a fork in the path. She called back over her shoulder.

"We'll be late for dinner, won't we? It's faster this way."

Picking up speed, she had passed a number of trees before he was able to catch up with her.

He walked beside her for a while then, looking at her sideways, he finally asked, "Working up an appetite?"

"You could say that."

The candle between them fluttered as a waiter passed their table, its glow reflected in the window that overlooked the gardens. Adam watched the play of light on Frances's face as she moved, thinking how even though there was tiredness around her eyes, she'd never looked more beautiful to him. *Maybe it's because I've got her to myself,* he thought. The pre-dinner drink, and now the shiraz, had helped to relax her after her sudden agitation in the gardens. Frances steered the discussion towards Adam, displaying a keen interest in his life and interests. Eventually, he began talking about his marriage.

"She hated it…the whole thing."

"What did she hate?"

"The music. The life—oh, I know it was hard on her, me being on stage three or four times a week."

"But surely she knew to expect that when you married?"

"I don't think she gave it any serious thought. She loved the social whirl, but she wanted it every night. I just couldn't be there." He grinned ruefully. "She would've been happier if I'd been a doctor, I think."

"They have night calls too," Frances smiled.

"So they do!" he laughed, before growing serious again. "Melanie was so…explosive! I'm surprised my violin survived the marriage."

"What do you mean?"

"She would've loved to use it for firewood. 'That useless lump of wood', she called it. Threatened to chop it up and burn it. I was obsessed near the end. Took to locking it in the boot of my car just in case. Wouldn't you?"

Frances looked shocked as she nodded in agreement.

He continued. "One night she threw a pile of sheet music into the fire. We were having one of our many arguments. She said, 'You spend more time between these sheets than the ones on our bed!' Can you imagine? It was something I'd been composing for years. I watched it burn and thought: just like our marriage—up in smoke. Lucky I had it up here," he said pointing to his head, "and was able to remember most of it. It was almost finished back then, but I didn't have any reason to go on with it. I wrote it all down again but just couldn't finish the last movement." He said with mock pride, "It was to be the greatest violin concerto since Tchaikovsky's."

He stopped to take a sip of his wine. There was an awkward silence between them.

Finally Frances said, "Well, then, will you play it for me?"

"Here?" He pretended to look under the table for his violin.

"No, silly," she laughed.

"But it's not finished," he protested.

"Why don't you try again? Maybe you can regain your creative spirit."

"With you to inspire me, I'm sure I can."

She laughed nervously in an effort to hide her embarrassment. "I don't know about that."

"I do."

The waiter interrupted with the wine bottle, refilling their glasses. Frances found it difficult to meet Adam's gaze.

"You must have been a source of pride for your parents," he said when the waiter left them alone again.

"Not at all."

"Why not? You're successful, intelligent…beautiful."

"Adam! Stop it!" She was glad it was too dark for him to see her blush.

"I only speak the truth, mademoiselle."

The waiter returned with their main course and they ate in silence for a few moments before Adam resumed the conversation.

"Do they live in Melbourne?"

"No."

"Where, then?"

"In Queensland. On the coast."

"Great spot for holidays! Near Surfers?"

"No. Redcliffe."

"Not so many tourists up that way. I suppose you enjoy getting up to the sunshine?"

"No. Never," she said to her plate.

"Oh?"

She looked up. "They never wanted me, you see. I was a nuisance. An accident."

Adam stared at her. She looked upset as she picked at the hem of the tablecloth.

"What sort of accident?"

"Pardon?"

"You said you were an accident," he persisted.

"Oh…it's the truth," she said, still picking at the tablecloth. "I wasn't exactly what you'd call a planned baby. I hardly knew them. They travelled so much. And, when they were at home, I was expected to stay out of sight. Out of mind."

Adam waited for her to go on. She released the tablecloth and took another sip of wine.

"People would come to the house. Other musicians. They would play. And I would watch them from the stairs, wishing I could be a part of their life. I wasn't allowed. It felt like I spent most of my childhood in my room…alone." She swallowed hard. "I had no-one to play with. Even the servants kept their children away." She paused and then spoke in a whisper, "I don't think they liked me."

He saw that her memories brought her pain but he listened in silence, wanting to know more, afraid that if he interrupted she would stop.

"There were no family picnics, no family celebrations. Just…emptiness." She looked at him with a forced smile, her eyes bright with unshed tears. "But I had my books. The characters were my friends. I shared my secrets with them. They lived in my world."

Hurt now showed plainly on her face.

"My mother would sometimes come to my room. She would pretend to kiss me. But there was no love in it. When she walked out her perfume would linger. It would stay there long after she'd gone. I remember taking it into my nostrils and holding my breath, keeping her there longer." She looked down at her hands before continuing. "You know, my father hardly ever spoke to me. It was like I never existed for him. He resented me. He was completely dedicated to his career—and to Mother."

She took up her glass with a shaking hand and looked out of the window, seeing nothing but the past in the darkness outside. He wondered if she felt any relief in the letting-out of her story.

"Why Melbourne?"

"It was far enough away," she said matter-of-factly.

She stood up.

"I'm sorry." Her voice shook. "I'm just going to the bathroom."

"Are you all right?"

"Yes. I won't be a minute."

He stood up, looking after her, then resumed his seat. He thought how effectively she constructed a façade over her soul. Watching her walking towards the bathroom, she appeared the most poised, sophisticated, relaxed person in the restaurant, and yet he suspected that her being was melting in torment.

Frances spent quite some minutes leaning against the wall of the toilet cubicle, trying to stop the trembling of her body and the riot of emotions she was feeling. She'd never, never, told anyone about her parents—not even Samuel. Why was she telling Adam, of all people, who she hardly knew? She felt raw, exposed, hurt. And it had been her own doing. She had unleashed a torrent of memories that she had neatly tucked away, out of sight and mind, never permitting them the luxury of performing upon her conscious stage. Of course she knew that she had no control over her sub-conscious—that those memories plagued concert performances which echoed her parents' music; that her dreams were filled with distorted versions of the truth. But to summon the voices and pain from the past, to present them like items on the menu, was sheer madness.

You go back, she told herself, *and act like any normal human being. Smile—and stop being such a wet blanket!*

She flushed the toilet and walked over to a basin. The cool water felt refreshing on her hands and she splashed her face with it, gasping a little with the shock of it. A long and searching look at her reflection in the mirror as she composed herself, showed a face that looked cool and emotionless.

Suddenly the bathroom door banged open and a woman entered. Frances regarded her friend, Gail, with surprise in the mirror.

"Gail! What are you doing here?"

"I might ask you the same thing, you dark horse."

"What do you mean?"

They hugged and Gail stood back to admire Frances.

"That gorgeous male out there who's been devouring you with his eyes all night."

Frances blushed. "Adam? Yes, he is rather handsome."

"Handsome! He's magnificent! Where've you been hiding him all this time? No wonder you didn't want to go out with Bob. And forget Samuel!"

"It's not like that."

"It should be!" She looked at Frances keenly. "Finally."

Uncomfortable with Gail's directness, Frances changed the subject. "I didn't see you out there."

"We're on the other side of the restaurant. I tried to catch your eye, but you were too busy impressing Mr Wonderful. Can't blame you, though."

"Oh, Gail," Frances laughed, despite herself, "you're insane!"

"Well, come on," Gail prodded, as she went into a cubicle. She banged the door shut behind her and called out, "Who, what and how?"

Frances smiled to herself at Gail's persistence. "Well…" she said to the cubicle, "he's a musician…a violinist."

"Ten points for that one!"

"I've not known him very long."

"But you will. Has he proposed yet?"

"Don't be ridiculous!"

"Or have you proposed to him?"

"I'm not in the habit of…"

"Is he married?"

"Divorced."

"Children?"

"Not that I know of."

"Good. Less complicated that way. No step-sibling rivalry when you start producing your own tribe."

"Will you stop?"

The toilet flushed and Gail reappeared.

"You must introduce me!" she said as she washed her hands.

"Only if you behave yourself," Frances said sternly.

Gail held her hand over her heart. "I swear. You know me."

"Yes, I do. That's what I'm worried about."

"Come on. I'm dying to meet him."

At the door, Frances held Gail back by the arm, suddenly serious. There was fear in her eyes. "Please. Don't embarrass me."

Also serious, Gail replied, "I promise. I won't spoil it for you. I want to see you happy. It's about time."

"Look—I'm only out to dinner with him. And I don't want him to get the wrong idea about me."

"I really hope he does."

"I don't want to put him under any pressure."

"Him…or you?"

Frances looked at her friend for a long moment. "I…I…"

"Give him a chance. Don't blow this one."

"I don't…"

"Let him in, Frances."

They walked towards the table where Adam was seated. He stood as they neared.

"Gail, I'd like you to meet Adam Harcourt. Adam, this is Gail Jennings, an old friend of mine."

"Pleased to meet you, Gail. Won't you join us?"

"No, thanks. My friend's waiting for me over there," she said waving in the direction of a table on the other side of the restaurant. "Probably thinks I've left him."

"Perhaps he'd like to join us too?"

"No," she said regretfully. "Two's company—but four's a crowd. You don't want us to ruin your night." She noticed Frances frown, so she changed the subject. "Enjoying the food?"

"Yes," he nodded.

"Frances tells me you're the concertmaster with the symphony?"

"Yes, I'm lucky. They're a bunch of very talented musicians."

"Hope I can see you perform sometime."

"I hope so."

"I'll ring you soon, Frances, and we can make a night of it. Dennis," she said nodding in the direction of her table, "likes classical music. We could have dinner first—or is that difficult for you, Adam?"

"It is a bit. But supper afterwards would be great."

Frances looked uncomfortable. "Perhaps Adam wouldn't like…"

"Of course he would, wouldn't you, Adam?"

"Most definitely," he agreed.

"She doesn't get out much, this recluse friend of mine. How did you drag her out of prison?"

"With great difficulty!"

"I can imagine. Where's the old boy?"

"Gail!"

"I thought he was super-glued onto you. Are you sure he's not under the table?"

Adam smothered a smile, but Frances laughed outright. "You shouldn't talk about him like that!"

Adam feigned ignorance. "Samuel?"

"Who else," Gail giggled. "God's gift to men."

"Samuel's a wonderful man," Frances said in his defence.

"Yes, we all know that, dear. But he normally won't let you out of his sight. Is he sick tonight or something?"

"No…"

"Oh, I get it," she said slowly. "He doesn't know about this little tête-à-tête?"

"Not exactly," Frances admitted. "But I don't have to justify myself to Samuel."

"You know, Adam," Gail said earnestly. "It's good to see her out and about—without the old boy. You should do it more often."

"I'd like that very much," he said warmly, taking a liking to Gail.

"I've tried for years to get her out—wouldn't even go away to Bali with me. I mean…what better company could she want? You must have something I don't!"

"Only Frances can answer that."

"I really think…"

"It's all right, Frances," Gail laughed. "I'll go. Dennis'll be on the third bottle of port by now—I'd better go and help him with it."

"I'll talk to you soon," Frances said, hugging her friend.

Gail turned to Adam, holding out her hand. "Nice meeting you, Adam."

"You too," he said bending over her hand.

Her eyebrows shot up in surprise. She mouthed 'Wow' over his head at Frances. "Great teeth," she nodded in approval as he smiled at her. He laughed easily in response.

They both watched her make her way around the tables and say something quickly to her companion who looked in their direction and waved. Frances and Adam waved back.

"She's a bubbly type. I like her," he said.

"Yes…she's fun, but genuine. We've been friends almost since I first moved to Melbourne."

Most of the tension had been worked out of her by Gail's infectious personality and the successful meeting of her friend with Adam. They bent over their deserts in a comfortable silence.

Frances found his eyes upon her every time she looked up. She couldn't see their colour in the dim candle light but she could almost swear he was making love with them. *He's looking at my mouth!* Her spoon stopped half-way between her lips and she withdrew it, licking her lips nervously. *He* is *looking at it!*

Adam's focal point roved slowly across her face, taking in every detail, wishing he could touch it. He remembered the feel of her lips on his, the surge inside him as she had responded so briefly, and he felt the surge again as he saw her lick her lips. A nerve pulsed in her neck like a ripple on the surface of a pond, betraying hidden life underneath. He wished he could place his lips—ever so lightly—upon the pulse, so that its fluttering would reach into him.

The waiter suddenly appeared with a complimentary glass of liqueur each. The spell was broken for a while as they sipped their drinks, the strong amber liquid like fire on the insides of their mouths, then burning languidly into their throats.

Adam slowly reached over the table and took her hand. She took in a sharp breath and went to pull her hand back, but he held onto it until she gradually relaxed, leaving it inside his. He willed her to leave it there with his eyes, smiling at her. She saw the corners of his mouth turned up, causing the deep lines beside it to echo his smile. His eyes were soft, compelling. Her hand felt small and protected inside his own. It felt a warmth that reached a place deep inside her—a place that had never been reached before.

Chapter 18

It was not until they realised that they were the only diners left in the restaurant that they reluctantly got up to leave. Frances wished they could have stayed there forever, chatting softly over the candlelight, holding hands, drinking in each other's companionship. If they didn't have to leave and return to normality, there would be no tomorrow, no complications.

They crossed Clarendon Street and began walking through the hushed gardens. Adam offered her his arm and she took it willingly.

"I really would like to see those trees, you know," he said carefully.

There was no answer other than a tightening of her arm.

He looked at her. "You're not in a hurry now, are you?"

"No..."

"Then how about it?"

"If you must."

Her lips were tight and she released his arm. The closeness between them had been shattered and he wondered, with regret, if he should have insisted. They walked on in silence until they neared a row of Moreton Bay figs.

Here, sinister shadows played around the base of the trees. Adam stopped at the largest of them. Frances hung back on the path, looking about her anxiously.

"This is it?" he asked, his voice instinctively hushed.

Frances stepped back further, her face lost in shadow. He saw her nod, missing the look of alarm on her face. He looked up at the canopy where the moonlight shone through it, casting speckled shadows over him like a black and white kaleidoscope, as he moved underneath. Walking around the tree, he marvelled at the shape of the roots, how he could walk into them and be almost concealed from the casual observer. He looked back at Frances's dim shape still in the same place and decided to enter one of the root cavities.

"You could hide in here," he mumbled to himself.

He waited for her to join him but she remained where she was. Running his hands along the roots, he found the bark cracking into small pieces and absentmindedly picked at them as he explored the roots.

Frances watched him, at once horrified and fascinated, as the tree took on a ghostly quality. It appeared like a photograph in negative, where the images are switched back to front and hidden aspects take on an unnatural prominence. She saw a man, his face indistinct, as he emerged from the tree roots and came towards her.

Panic heaved inside her. She screamed as she turned away from the tree and her feet flew along the path. Adam shouted after her but it didn't register upon her terrified mind. She heard, instead, a roaring of wind and rain, even though the night was mild and still. Her heart pumped loudly in her ears, along with the roaring, but she became aware of footsteps running after her. Pounding footsteps. Gaining upon her. The roaring became louder. She screamed again as a hand grabbed her arm.

Coming to a halt, she felt her body being turned. Fighting, hitting, screaming, at last she focused on Adam's face. Sobbing with relief and falling onto her knees, he knelt with her, holding her, as she sobbed into his arms.

My God, what have I done? he berated himself.

They walked back to Frances's apartment in silence, and mounted the few steps to the security door with his arm draped protectively around her shoulders. The lift rose soundlessly to her floor. They looked at each other in the mirrored walls and she shrank away from him, embarrassed at the picture of their closeness in the reflection. He dropped his arm slowly to his side. Her hand shook as she tried to insert her key into her door. His hand slid over hers to guide the key into the hole. They turned it together, the lock clicking faintly, and they both stood looking at the cactus on the hall table as the door swung open.

Adam poured brandy into a glass and took it over to the couch where Frances was resting against a pile of cushions he'd pushed behind her. She sipped at it gratefully, trying to control the shaking of her hands. He saw a little colour bleed into her pallid face.

"I'm so sorry," he said, sitting down beside her. "I shouldn't have made you go there."

"It's not your fault," she said weakly.

"I could kick myself." He looked at her closely. "I wouldn't hurt you for the world."

She took another sip without answering. He could see she was calming down slowly.

"Frances?"

"Umm…?"

"What *is* it about those trees?"

She sighed. "I don't know."

"But you *must* have some idea."

"No, I don't."

"Anything?"

She was emphatic. "No."

"Those trees hold the clue to whatever's upsetting you," he insisted, hoping he wasn't going too far.

She looked at him in stony silence.

"Do you want to talk about it?"

"No."

"Why not? Don't you trust me?"

"It's not that. I just don't want to talk about it."

"Something must have happened…"

"I think it would be best if you go now." Her tone was brittle.

"You'd rather be alone?"

"It's not that. I just…"

"What?"

"I don't think we should see each other anymore."

A look of intense pain crossed his face. "I'm sorry if I…"

"I can't give you what you want."

"I'm not asking for anything!"

"No—but you will."

Her face was stiff, cold.

"It's the trees, isn't it?"

"No!"

"What *is* it?"

He grabbed her hands, forcing her to look at him.

"Think, Frances! Think! What hurt you?"

Breaking away from him, she struggled to her feet. He stood up beside her.

Bursting into tears, she cried, "Leave me alone!"

"All right." His tone was grim. "But I'm not giving up." He tried to take her hand again, but she shook him off. "I'll ring you."

"Please don't."

"You'll have to face it sometime."

"No!"

Frances walked deliberately to the door and held it open. They looked at each other across the room, then he walked reluctantly towards her. The muscles of his face worked. Tense, he felt coiled up like a spring.

He suddenly reached out and put his arms around her, pulling her roughly to him. He buried his face in her neck, stealing in her perfume as she sagged against him, then she struggled and pushed him away. As they separated, he slammed his fist against the wall in frustration. She jumped, startled, eyes wide. It took him some moments to control himself, his forehead against the wall, his breathing ragged. Finally he turned to face her. An uncomfortable silence isolated them as they regarded each other. Her eyes were wary.

Her voice was a whisper. "Please go."

"I'm only a phone call away."

"I know."

He walked through the doorway and she closed the door quickly behind him. Leaning against it, she cried tears of sheer helplessness until she slid down to the floor.

She stared at her lounge room, now so empty. He had filled it with his personality so easily, so completely. And now she felt a heavy loneliness that she had never felt before, seeping into her skin, weighing her down, and turning her gut into a painful mass.

Plato joined her there, rubbing his head against her hand, wanting her to caress him. He'd been enough for her before, she'd told herself, but somehow his company just wasn't enough at that very moment.

She asked herself how could such a beautiful night have gone so wrong. Why did she behave the way she did? What was it that set her off in such a panic? Why couldn't she just accept what she thought Adam was trying to offer her—even if only friendship? Any *normal* woman—yes, normal—would be flattered by the attentions of a man like Adam. My God, he was so handsome, so talented, so charming—just so damned wonderful. Gail had seen it in such a short space of time. Why couldn't she, Frances, let him in, as Gail had insisted? It was like a guardian rejecting anybody if they got too close. Their friendship would be destroyed by it and she would continue on as always in her rotten, shallow existence—*yes, admit it!*—pushing them aside. You don't get hurt that way, she told herself. *Don't let them in. Don't let them in. Don't let them in.*

Chapter 19

The mild, still night gave way to blustering rain clouds in the early hours of the morning. The canopy of trees below Frances's apartment was flung in frenzied abandon. The gardens' bird life took shelter as best it could.

A shadowy figure walked up the driveway and rang Frances's doorbell. His features were indistinct in the darkness; his clothes dripped from the thorough soaking he'd received since stepping out of his car. One hand was behind his back. He waited and then pressed the doorbell again. He heard a crackling as Frances's voice came through the speaker.

"Who is it?"

"Frances, it's me. Adam."

"Oh, please! I told you…"

"I just want to show you something."

"Please, Adam. Leave me alone."

"Not until you come down here."

"No!"

There was a click and then silence. He put his ear to the speaker and listened for a moment, then pushed the doorbell again.

"I told you. Go away!"

"Not until you come down here."

Frances clicked off again. Adam wiped water out of his eyes as he poked at the doorbell again. He listened and, when she failed to reply, he jammed his finger onto the bell and left it there.

"Frances?"

He pushed the bell again.

"I'm not giving up." He waited. "You'll have to come out sometime." No sound came from the speaker. "And I'll still be here." He called out more loudly. "I'm getting awfully wet." A moment passed then, "I might catch a cold and die."

He took his hand away from the doorbell and leaned against the wall, out of the rain, prepared to wait as long as it took. After a few minutes the door opened with a bang and Frances stormed out, nearly crashing into him. The wind whisked her hair back from her face as she pulled her dressing gown close to her chest against the cold.

"Why can't you leave me alone?" She was furious.

"Because I love you," he whispered.

"What do you want of me?" she shouted against the wind.

"I just want to show you something."

His arm came around from behind his back holding an axe. Frances's eyes widened as she saw the glint of the head in the light from the doorway. She stepped back in alarm.

"My God! Are you mad?"

Without a word, he turned and walked back down the stairs and into the rain.

"What are you doing?" she screamed at him in fear.

He crossed the road without looking back and entered the gardens, taking the path that led past the row of fig trees where they had been earlier that night. Frances poked her head around the corner of the entrance, staggering back from a blast of wind and rain. Gasping at the cold and the sudden drenching, she looked behind her at the security door that stood ajar, then she put her head around the corner again. She could just make out Adam's figure in the rain.

He's gone berserk!

Hesitating for a moment, she bent her head against the rain and ran down the steps after him. In seconds her dressing gown clung to her; she shivered as she crossed the road. Adam was walking faster now. She had to hurry to catch up with him. He stopped as he reached the largest of the fig trees. She saw him brace himself and then swing the axe above his head in a wide arc before coming down upon one of the root walls.

"Stop," she screamed at him. "Stop!"

He struggled with the axe head in the root, then turned to look at her over his shoulder. "Why should I stop? Why?"

The axe came out of the root suddenly and he staggered to regain his balance. Then he began to chop at the roots rhythmically. Half-blinded by the pelting rain, Frances attempted to grab his arm. With each impact, her body shuddered as if struck. He continued swinging the axe into the tree roots, ignoring her attempts to stop him. Her fingers slipped as water flew off his arm, and she fell backwards onto the ground. She gasped as she looked up, the rain stinging her face.

The roots rose up hugely around her, like monstrous twisted black eels. They appeared to writhe with each blow of the axe giving glimpses of a frightened face emerging from behind them.

"Stop," she screamed up at him, her voice cracking.

He paused, panting from his exertions.

"Please," she begged him. "Please."

"Not until you confront your nightmare," he shouted.

She got up off the ground, heedless of the mud clinging to her dressing gown and legs. Despite a feeling of revulsion, she backed up against the tree roots, her hands running over the wet cracked walls.

"You can't do this," she shrieked at him.

His hands left the handle of the axe and took hold of her waist. He pulled her away from the tree and looked at her frantic eyes for a moment before pushing her onto the path.

"I'm going to destroy it," he shouted, as he pulled the axe out of the root and began swinging at it again.

"You can't!" She looked back along the path. "You'll be arrested."

His gaze followed hers and he shrugged. "By whom?" He looked back at her, his face grim. "I'm going to chop this bloody thing down if you won't try to remember."

"I can't."

"You won't, you mean!"

"I can't!"

"You can!" The axe head buried deep into the root. "Face it, Frances." He pulled it out and swung again. "Face it!"

"Nooo…"

"Whose hands were they, Francis? Can you see them now? Can you feel them?"

He chopped at the roots, furiously now.

"It's the tree," he shouted at her. "Look at it. Look! What do you see? *Who* do you see?"

She looked in confusion between Adam and the tree. The wind and rain howled in her mind, creating kaleidoscopic images that clouded her vision. She no longer knew where she was, or who she was looking at. His hair was plastered around his head, changing the shape of what she knew to be Adam. A stranger stood in front of her, eyes screwed up against the rain, panting, holding onto the axe.

Terror roared through her as the stranger turned back to the tree. Her eyes took in the threatening movement of his broad back and powerful muscles with each swing of the axe. Suddenly she was running, her breath rasping in her throat, her heart pounding in her chest. Running wildly, her sodden slippers ripped from her feet, making her stumble. She regained her balance and resumed her flight towards her apartment, crying hysterically.

At first Adam was not aware that Frances had run off as he continued to chop at the tree. When he paused for breath, he looked around in time to see her running along the path. He stood back gasping from his exertions, the axe head embedded in the root. Rain pelted the leaves of the tree, its weight pointing them towards the ground. It stained the trunk and branches, and snaked its way darkly down the roots, scurrying around the gaping wound from where the axe head violated the now-broken rampart.

"Oh, Jesus!" he gasped as Frances disappeared from sight.

He left the axe and ran after her. At the end of the path, he caught a glimpse of her as she stumbled up the steps. He saw her grab the handrail and steady herself before going through the doorway. As he reached the foot of the steps, the security door slammed shut, leaving a trail of water behind her. He stood panting as a stitch dug painfully into his side. Rivulets of water surged along choked gutters, splashing over clumps of leaves, sodden discarded paper, and dodging car tyres parked in their way. His feet squelched inside his water-filled shoes and he looked down surprised to see that he was standing in a puddle.

When Adam had recovered enough strength to climb the steps, he leaned against the wall before jamming his finger on Frances's doorbell. He pressed it once, twice, and again, but there was no answer. He turned and slowly descended the steps and walked back into the rain to retrieve the axe.

The steam from the running shower filled the bathroom and spilled out into Frances's bedroom. Hot water ran in a steady stream on her naked body as she scrubbed frantically at her already-raw skin.

The phone rang in her bedroom but, with the noise of the shower running, she was unaware of its insistent ringing. It stopped and rang again for a while before it stopped once more.

Twenty minutes later, Frances emerged from the bathroom with a towel wrapped around her hair. She was shivering from the water that had turned cold. Plato followed her into the kitchen where she took two tablets from the bottle of herbal sleeping pills. His eyes watched her hand hesitate over the lid as she began to screw it shut, then undo it again and shake out a small handful. He padded silently behind her as she re-entered the bathroom and took a hairdryer out of a drawer. As she turned it on, the phone rang again, too late for her to hear it. Plato looked at the phone in the bedroom and then at Frances, then went back into the kitchen looking in vain at his empty feed bowl. He hated the sound of the hairdryer.

Just before dawn, when the birds in Fitzroy Gardens were about to unfold their wings after their brief snatch of sleep since the storm had abated, a scream slashed through the quiet. The lamp beside Frances's bed suddenly burst into light, casting its glow through the doorway of her bedroom. She dashed into the lounge room.

"Adam! Adam!"

Looking wildly around the dim room, she realised he wasn't there.

"Oh, God," she cried, clinging to the couch. "Help me."

Slowly she sank to her knees and sat on the floor looking dumbly out of the french doors as the first rays of light percolated through them.

The coffee plunger stood empty beside her mug on the kitchen table. Her mouth tasted foul as she ran her tongue absentmindedly over her teeth. Her eyes felt like they were moving in sand, and she could barely support her head that was propped up by a hand at her chin. Afraid to return to her nightmare, she stayed there watching the second hand of the kitchen clock going around and around.

The phone rang and she jumped at its loud clatter. She turned her head slowly away from the clock face to look at the phone. It continued to ring as she watched it, wondering why it wouldn't stop. Its reverberations filled the room, clanging in her head painfully as if they would burst it. Then, just as suddenly, it relinquished its hold upon her ears and its echoes faded like a memory.

She sat there oblivious to her surroundings, frozen in a misery that was beyond her understanding.

Chapter 20

Samuel looked up in surprise when he heard Frances's key open the door of *The Bookcase*. He walked into the public space from the back room to see her walking towards him, her eyes circled darkly and her face pale, drawn.

"Where have you been?"

"At home."

"I've been ringing…I don't know how many times. I even went to your place and rang the doorbell. I've been frantic." His voice rose. "I was going to get the police to break the door down."

"We are *only* business partners, Samuel."

He looked at her strangely, startled by her tone.

"Do you expect me to run the shop by myself?" he demanded.

She stood unmoving, regarding him in silence.

"Hello?" He snapped his fingers in front of her face. "Anyone home?"

He was greeted with a continuing silence; anger rose hotly inside him.

"This is ridiculous! What's the matter with you?"

"Nothing," she said finally.

"If there's nothing the matter, why do you look and act like a zombie?"

"Excuse me?"

"You heard."

"Why are you being so nasty?"

"What do you expect? I've had to do all the work around here for the past two days!" He glared at her. "Are you here to work or not?"

"Yes, of course I am."

She sat on the edge of the counter and yawned.

"You can't work like this," he exploded.

"Just watch me," she said evenly.

They both looked up as the doorbell rang and a customer entered. Samuel turned back to Frances, giving her a long searching look, before going over to the customer to offer assistance.

It had been a long, busy day. One of those days when nothing seemed to go right and each customer appeared to be in a belligerent mood—possibly because the vibes coming from a put-out Samuel and an exhausted Frances did little to enhance the atmosphere in *The Bookcase*. They always took their lunch breaks at separate times, so that there was always someone in the shop, but mostly they took just enough time to eat their lunch out in the back room, and then joined the other in the shop. This time, however, when the shop was free of customers, Frances took her sandwich over to the gardens.

Samuel watched her cross the road and disappear behind a clump of bushes. He ground his teeth together in resentment. *That's right, leave me to do everything.* He tidied the counter roughly, slamming books down and picking them up again. *I'll have it out with her.* He dropped a book onto the floor, and bent to retrieve it, carefully bending back the edges where it had landed. "Shit!" He frowned. He hated any damage to books. It cost money. *She'll just have to go and see a shrink.* The front cover of the book had creased. *She's putting the business in jeopardy.*

Frances sat on a bench in the gardens, her sandwich untouched on her lap. Her mind was in turmoil but she pushed all thoughts aside and concentrated instead upon the bird life around her. She watched a family of Indian Mynas as they foraged for food, the diligent parents instructing their young in the skills that would be essential for their survival once out of the nest. Not slow to react, the father of the family picked up a piece of bread Frances broke off from her sandwich and returned with it to his young to peck at. They looked at her expectantly when they finished it, hopping around on the grass in front of her. She managed a smile and threw them the rest of her sandwich.

"You're a lot hungrier than I am," she said softly as she got up to leave.

For the umpteenth time, Frances glanced at her watch as she finished serving a customer. Even though the afternoon had been a busy one, time had dragged for her. She was relieved to see that they would be closing in a few minutes. Samuel was already walking towards the door to turn the lock. It was obvious he'd been trying to talk to her, but she'd managed to avoid him so far. If she got out of the shop fast enough, he would have to leave it. She'd go home, have a long soak in the bath while playing a relaxing CD, take some sleeping pills and have an early night. *If I have a good night's sleep, I'll be like new tomorrow*, she tried to convince herself.

Just then the door opened and a young man walked in. There was something familiar about him, but it wasn't until the smell of beer wafted over to Frances, that she recognised him as the inebriated man who had made a nuisance of himself some weeks back. He looked tidier than the time before. He was well groomed, dressed in a suit, but obviously had been drinking again. Samuel took one look at Frances's expression of disgust and realised that it was the same man who had caused such a drastic reaction before.

"I'm sorry, sir," he said, blocking the young man's way. "We're just closing."

The man tore his gaze from Frances and focused upon Samuel. "Oh, come on, mate," he whined.

Samuel's tone was icy. "Was it something urgent, sir?"

"Yeah. I wanna buy a book. You're a book shop, aren't you?"

Frances looked with distaste from the customer to Samuel, shaking her head.

"I'm sorry, but we're closing now," Samuel said firmly. "I must ask you to leave. We open at nine tomorrow."

The phone rang and Frances picked it up, keeping her eyes on Samuel.

"Good afternoon. This is *The Bookcase*. How can I help you?"

She frowned as she listened, then she turned her back and perched on the edge of the counter as she held the receiver to her ear. Her voice was low as she responded. Samuel saw that her knuckles were white as she gripped the phone. He was puzzled at the stiffness of her body, the tension that emanated from her. *It's that Harcourt again. He's the cause of all this.*

"She your missus?" The customer's voice was close to Samuel's ear.

"Yes. Yes," Samuel replied impatiently. "Now I'm locking the door."

He held the door open, finding it hard to resist the impulse to push the annoying man out into the street. He glanced back at Frances, curious to know what was causing such close attention. He strained his ears to catch what she was saying, but the customer continued to interrupt.

"No hard feelings, mate."

"There will be if you don't get out—now!"

"Okay. Okay." The young man held up his hands in surrender. "I'm going."

He lurched out of the door, giving a rueful backward glance at Frances, before the door closed and the lock clicked noisily behind him.

Samuel checked through the window that the man was making his way along the street then turned to Frances. She was even more pale than before and trembling violently. He saw the receiver dangling off the hook, swinging slowly back and forth behind the counter. She was staring fixedly at it.

Samuel stood as the doctor came out of Frances's bedroom and closed the door quietly behind him. He took a stethoscope from around his neck and put it in his bag.

"She won't wake up until morning."

Samuel looked relieved. "Good. She needs sleep desperately."

"Can you be here when she wakes up?"

"Don't worry. I'll sleep on the couch. She won't get past me."

"She can't go to the funeral alone, you know. She's not well enough."

Samuel looked out of the window thoughtfully. "Yes, I know. It's been building up for some time and I think her mother's death has just capped it off."

"You'll go with her?"

"I don't think I'm the right person," he said slowly, "but I know someone who would be."

Samuel poured himself a drink and sat staring at the floor, his drink untouched. His thoughts whirled in tortured chaos. *Just what is it about him I don't like?* At last he was prepared to look at himself honestly. *You're jealous. But is that fair to her?* He picked with disgust at a strand of cat's fur that had attached itself to his trouser leg. *Can I hold onto her forever?*

He took a long swig of his drink and went over to Frances's desk. His hand covered the receiver of the telephone for some time before picking it up. The dial tone sounded loud in his ear. He looked down at the numbers and slowly punched ten digits.

An hour later, he opened the door to Adam.

"What'd you do, come by helicopter?"

Adam grinned. "Something like that. I wasn't far away."

"Well, thanks," Samuel grunted, leading the way into the lounge room.

He poured a drink for each of them and then sat down opposite Adam. They both looked at the closed bedroom door and instinctively lowered their voices.

"As I said to you on the phone," Samuel said, taking a sip of his drink, "she's just not well enough to travel…well, not on her own."

"And you really think that I should be the one to go?"

Samuel nodded. "But, you've got your work commitments…what about them?"

"I can fix that."

"Good."

Samuel got up from his chair and started pacing the room. He stopped suddenly and sat down again, leaning towards Adam across the coffee table.

"I guess you know I lied. About the marriage…"

Adam opened his mouth to speak, but Samuel silenced him with a gesture of the hand.

"No, hear me out." He paused, gathering his thoughts. "It was stupid. Wrong. I pushed my luck a bit too far that time."

Adam received the doubtful apology with tight lips, obviously still feeling a bit miffed about it, but at the same time feeling pity for the older man who had felt the need to resort to such a low trick.

"You know," Samuel continued, "I think the world of Frances. I've been so lucky! I have this beautiful woman for a business partner, *The Bookcase* is going ahead in leaps and bounds, and I have Frances to be seen with in the right places. We even share the same taste in music!"

Plato sidled into the room from the kitchen and rubbed up against Adam's leg. Samuel looked quickly at Frances's bedroom door and lowered his voice even further.

"Can't stand cats, though. Never told her. She loves the stupid thing too much."

Adam laughed and picked up the cat, where it settled down contentedly on his lap. The sound of purring was loud in the quiet room.

"She's made me face up to a few things lately." Samuel tossed the rest of his drink down. "I've been selfish. Expected too much of our relationship." He pulled a face as he ran a finger around the rim of his empty glass. "She reminded me the other day that we are only business partners. Nothing more. Well I knew that, didn't I? We are the best of friends, though…or were."

He got up to refill his glass, raising an eyebrow to Adam who shook his head, not having touched his own drink. Samuel thought better of it and put his empty glass down on the coffee table and began to pace the floor again, pausing to look at Frances's door once more.

"But do you know what has always puzzled me?" he asked without waiting for a reply. "I couldn't understand why she didn't have men falling all over her. I mean—*any* man would want her, wouldn't he?"

Adam nodded in agreement.

"But it didn't take me long to figure out that she needed protection from men. She wanted nothing to do with them. Well, it suited me, didn't it? My life has been fantastic since she walked into it. I can be the *real* me…"

He stopped, looking at Adam in mute appeal. They regarded each other in silence and eventually Adam nodded knowing what Samuel was saying about his sexuality.

"…and still look respectable. But I must admit that it worried me. It pricked at my conscience. There's that lovely woman in there—unfulfilled. She deserves more in life than she's got. But there's something seriously wrong…isn't there?"

"I quite agree."

"She won't open up to me. Never has. About her past, that is. And that's where the problem is, I think. In her past."

"Yes."

Samuel rose an eyebrow in surprise. "She's told you?"

"A little."

He sat down again to look Adam squarely in the eyes. "Lately, something's getting under her skin. And I think you're part of it. Not that I think that's a bad thing—now."

"Why the change of heart?" Adam looked at him with suspicion.

"You're in love with her, aren't you?"

"Yes, I am."

"I thought so. And I think, in her own way, she loves you too. I think you're the only one that can help her. The only one she'll let in."

Chapter 21

Frances opened the door to Adam. He regarded her silently as he held a single long-stemmed rose out in front of him. She took it wordlessly and held it to her nose, looking at him over the flower. The deep red of the petals was in stark contrast to the pallor of her face which appeared like a porcelain mask with black smudges painted around the eyes. He noted there was no sign of tears, no trembling of the lips—no outward suggestion of grief except, perhaps, for the convention of the plain black dress she wore.

"Ready?" he asked softly.

She nodded and turned towards her small suitcase beside the hall table. Adam reached over, picked it up and they left the apartment without speaking. As they waited for the lift, they looked at each other in the mirrored surface of the doors. He wondered if she was really looking at him, or if she saw something else beyond the doors.

They entered the lift and waited as the slight falling sensation delivered them to the ground floor. They walked out of the building and along the street where Adam's car awaited them. He held the door open for her.

"Thank you," he heard her say.

She was still holding the rose.

Tullamarine Airport was alive with people to meet or farewell. The chaos of the check-in desk was claustrophobic and Frances shrank back, creating a space around herself that brooked no invasion. Adam took charge of booking in their meagre luggage, then took her arm and steered her away from the crowd to one of the bars overlooking the tarmac.

When they were seated, he asked, "Would you like a drink? A brandy perhaps?"

"Yes, that'd be nice," she responded.

"Anything else?"

"No." She shook her head. "Nothing, thanks."

"Have you eaten today?"

Her smile was bleak. "I don't think so."

Adam bought the drinks and returned to the table. Frances was studying the movement of workers and aircraft outside the plate glass windows.

"You wonder how they get them up in the air," she mused.

"I never understood that," he smiled. "Science was never one of my strengths."

"But music is."

"Yes."

"You're lucky." She sipped at her drink. "And very talented."

His eyebrows shot up at the compliment. "Well, thank you, Ma'am."

She turned back to the window, lost in thought. He was surprised at her composure, not having been sure what he would have to deal with. He'd had very little experience of death in his own family and, apart from old Mrs Lindberg—his blind friend—he'd so far escaped the pain of grief. He couldn't imagine what it must be like to lose a mother. Coming from a large family, he'd always felt he had a seventh share of his mother's attention—being six boys as well as his father—and wondered just how much she really did love him. She was the most caring, understanding, gentle human being, and he loved her unreservedly. He couldn't imagine life without her. Or the agony of no longer choosing a present for her on Mother's Day, or Christmas, or her birthdays. No matter what he had ever given her—what any of them gave her—she always took the time to examine and delight in it and make them feel it was the perfect gift— something she would have chosen herself. He found it hard to imagine her warm, soft body lying stiff on a mortuary slab, the eyes closed forever, the lips unmoving in speech or laughter. Or to imagine her resting inside the satin lining of a polished coffin as the thud of clods sounded on the closed lid. Nor could he imagine his father's grief at the empty space beside him in his bed.

Adam looked at Frances's profile; it betrayed nothing of her inner turmoil. He knew that she wasn't close to her mother — that her mother had never let her get close — and wondered if that made it easier for her to bear her mother's death. Perhaps she felt nothing after all. Perhaps it was like a stranger who'd died, and Frances just had to go through the motions of appearing at the funeral to support her father.

She looked around at Adam as she heard their flight called.

"That's us," she said quietly.

She looked into her glass as if the contents were the most interesting thing she'd seen all day.

She doesn't want to go.

"I haven't thanked you," she said suddenly.

"What for?" he asked, surprised.

"For coming with me."

"Oh, that's…"

"No. I really mean it." There was a faint suspicion of tears. "Thank you."

"You're very welcome."

The two hour flight to Brisbane was uneventful with Frances spending most of the time with ear phones on whilst staring out of the window. Adam knew she was listening to the classical channel because her fingers were moving in time to the Mozart symphony that he was listening to. She shook her head when the flight attendant handed her a lunch tray, keeping the table folded up at the back of the seat in front of her. Adam felt guilty eating his lunch but figured he'd be no use to her if he didn't eat and was concentrating on his empty stomach instead of her.

After they landed, he guided a hire car out of the airport complex and turned onto the Gateway Motorway. The humidity was high, oppressive, and they were glad of the air-conditioning in the car.

"This'd all be pretty familiar to you," he commented, pointing to their surroundings.

"Not really."

"Oh?"

"I hardly ever come to Queensland." She looked around her. "I didn't travel much as a child. My parents didn't bring me into Brisbane."

"Oh, I see."

"I could be a stranger to this city even though I spent the first eighteen years of my life here."

"Pity."

"It doesn't matter. Melbourne's my home."

They drove in silence for some time, turned onto the Old Cleveland Road, passed the Capalaba Shopping Centre, then arrived at the Cleveland Cemetery. Adam steered the car into a parking area and turned off the engine. He turned to Frances and saw her lips in a tight line, her jaw tense.

"Are you ready for this?" he asked gently.

She sighed. "I have no choice, have I?"

"No, you don't."

They got out of the car and Frances began to walk along a path that wound through the headstones.

"What about the service?" Adam asked.

"My father didn't want one," she replied. "It'll be at the gravesite."

Adam shrugged and fell into step beside her.

"Is that usual?"

"Possibly not. But then again, my parents are unusual people." She stopped as she saw a small group of people a few hundred yards away. "They make their own rules."

Adam was surprised to pick up faint strains of music caught on the breeze.

"Why, that's…"

"Albinoni. The *Adagio*," she finished for him. "Of course. Why didn't I think of that? I should have guessed."

"What?"

"The performance still goes on." Her tone was bitter.

They reached the gravesite where a shining mahogany coffin with ornate gold handles was suspended over a hole in the ground edged with synthetic grass. An elaborate arrangement of flowers draped the length of the coffin. Adam thought fleetingly of the cost of such an arrangement—it looked to him to be made up of exotic orchids and lilies, their colours luridly bright for the solemn occasion.

A priest stood at the head of the coffin, his white-laced robes flapping in the breeze that provided some relief from the hot sun. Perspiration gathered on his forehead; his thick dark hair was damp at the base of his neck where it curled over his tight collar.

Beside the grave was a quartet dressed formally—the women in long black skirts and deep violet bodices, and the men in tails and white shirts.

Adam judged there to be no more than twenty people standing solemnly around the gravesite, one of whom he recognised as Frances's father, Robert Draper. None of the group seemed to be aware of their arrival, but rather seemed to concentrate on the emotional atmosphere that the *Adagio* created in the hands of the quartet.

"All musicians," she whispered in Adam's ear. "Of course."

"No family?" he asked, just as softly.

Frances shook her head. "No one left."

They stood awkwardly as the piece continued uninterrupted, as though they were intruders upon the scene. Frances felt the situation grotesque, illusory, and yet she was not surprised. She wondered with shame what Adam was thinking as she worked her way through the group of people to her father's side. If he saw her approach, he failed to acknowledge it, until she leaned towards him in an attempt to kiss his cheek. He stiffened, then repelled her with a gesture, pointing towards the quartet, avoiding the contact. At his rebuff, a look of stunned hurt crept over her face before she had a chance to wipe it off. Her body swayed as the memory returned of her younger self being constantly rejected by her parents, blocking out the present. She was again at the foot of the stairs watching her parents as they created their musical world—without her. Once again she felt the sharp pang of exclusion, the loneliness of her childhood, the exile from a home she never had. The recurring nightmare of sinking into quicksand as her parents mouthed *Go away*, the receding stage that took her parents further from her, the drowning into nothingness, confused her mind so that she no longer knew if she was awake or living inside her nightmare. Tears welled in her eyes as she turned from the graveside and impulsively began to run.

Adam observed the pain reflected in Frances's face after she had attempted to kiss her father. He was horrified at the man's rejection of his daughter, at his coldness, his refusal to even acknowledge her, and his obsession with the quartet's playing. It made Adam feel ashamed that he himself was a musician, wondering at the bizarre farce being enacted in front of him. And what about the priest, he wondered, who appeared to be untouched by the scene, as was the rest of the group. It was as if Frances had no right to be there—was a mere annoyance, an interruption to the rite of music. And yet Robert Draper was not totally unaware, Adam noticed. The man's stiff demeanour was betrayed by a muscle twitching in his face, and his hands clenching and unclenching. But Adam knew the man was not trying to control tears; he was trying to control extreme irritation. As his daughter fled from his side, however, he remained focused upon the musicians with a determination Adam found disgusting.

The thought of his own mother's inevitable funeral, and the scene that he would be a part of, was completely different from what he was witnessing. He imagined his father's grief—his brothers' grief, as well as his own—and the support they would be for each other. He could see his sisters-in-law, aunts and uncles, his cousins, neighbours, friends, all beside them, all weeping for the loss of a generous and loving woman. He saw the close bond shared by all the mourners and heard the simple words of comfort that would be spoken by a celebrant. No—his mother's body would never rest in such a cold coffin, and it would be covered by the perfume and beauty of her favourite flowers.

These thoughts flashed through Adam's mind in mere seconds during the short time that Frances had approached her father. The hallucinatory effect of the scene played in slow motion through his consciousness, before he snapped into action to run after her. The dying strains of the *Adagio* accompanied her flight through the cemetery, its melancholy dripping over the headstones, a fitting epitaph for the departed.

She was some way ahead of him, running blindly between the headstones. The breeze captured the sound of her sobbing, flinging it back at him as he caught up with her. She stumbled and fell heavily on her knee and elbow. Blood oozed through a hole ripped in her pantyhose. He reached down to help her up. She looked dully at the hand he offered her, tears blurring her vision.

"Dad?" she whispered softly.

Adam's heart sank in sympathy. "I'm sorry," he said.

She blinked. "For a moment..."

He supported her as she got to her feet. "Are you badly hurt?"

Their eyes met before he folded his arms around her and her body sagged in defeat against him where she found comfort and kindness.

"Yes," she cried in answer, not thinking of her physical injuries.

As she sobbed into his chest, gradually releasing her pain and rejection to his now familiar calmness and patience, he understood what she meant. He looked over her head, as he stroked her back and shoulders, to see the musicians stand and join the rest of the group as the priest began his ritual. His eyes narrowed in anger as he realised that no one had taken any notice of Frances or the manner in which her father had rejected her. It was as if she didn't exist.

My God, he thought, *is this how she's always been treated?* His arms tightened around her protectively. *Her mother's dead, for Christ's sake! Don't they care about her daughter at all?* The realisation of what Frances must have suffered in her childhood dug into his belly. He remembered what she'd told him when they'd dined together, but seeing it happen had more impact upon him now. *The man needs hanging!*

Slowly, Adam led Frances away from the droning of the priest's voice as particles of the sermon shredded off into the wind. By the time they arrived back at the car, she was under control again, drained of emotion, crushed.

She sat looking out of the window, her face expressionless.

"Do you have to go to your father's house?"

It took her some time to answer. "It's probably expected."

That's what I thought. He stared grimly at the road ahead. He wondered if her fragile mind and body could stand any more.

Following her directions, he drove slowly, reluctantly, along a quiet tree-lined road. They seemed to be floating in the shadow of the canopy that flickered glances of sunlight through the leaves as they passed beneath.

Adam heard a sudden gasp beside him. He turned to see Frances with a look of utter horror on her face as she stared at the trees ahead. Braking hard, he brought the car to a stop just past the largest of the trees, which he realised was one of many huge Moreton Bay fig trees lining the road. She was looking back at it, her mouth open. It sounded as if she was having trouble breathing.

"Frances?" He looked back at the tree then reversed the car so that they were beside it. "What is it?" She shrank away from the window. "Is *that* the tree?"

A low moaning filled the car, setting his hair on end. Her face was turned away from him as she began to shake violently, pressing closer towards him. Instinctively his arms went around her, but he changed his mind and got out of the car and hurried around to her side. He opened the door and took hold of her arms, pulling her towards him.

"Frances, get out." His voice sounded harsh in his ears.

Her head shook violently as she cringed away from him, her eyes not leaving the tree in front of her.

He grabbed her more tightly. "Come on."

"No," she moaned. "No."

"It's time," he insisted, his voice loud. "Confront it now."

Her eyes left the tree to look in his face. What she saw there—patience, kindness, love—gave her the strength to reluctantly allow herself to get out of the car. He turned her towards the tree and she looked up to the shifting sunlight through the wide, dark green glossy leaves. Her vision began to spin as the scene turned to a negative image in black and white. She recoiled and struggled against him to get away.

"Don't run from it anymore," he said close to her ear as his arms encircled her tightly. "You have to do this."

"I can't. I can't. It's too horrible!"

"I'll bet it is. But try, Frances. Try!"

The long, thick branch stretches out reaching towards the road. Its upper surface is flat and wide so that Frances can sit on it safely. She is there for some time watching the birds flitting from branch to branch. Flashes of sunlight paint the birds' feathers in bright hues as the breeze moves the leaves. She gets up and walks back to the centre of the tree trunk above the roots where the open centre has an earthen floor. It is big enough to hold ten people and is hidden from view from below.

Adam's voice reached her faintly, as if losing volume through the space of years. "It was *this* tree?"

"Yes," she replied in a fearful, child-like voice.

A distortion dripped into her ears. "What's happening?"

"It's my special place," she whispered. "I bring books here when my parents are away." She sucked her breath in quickly. "I'm not allowed to come here."

"Why not?"

"So the servants won't have to come looking for me if I forget to go home."

The bark is cracked into tiny pieces inviting her small fingers to shred them off. She sits down and reads a book but becomes sleepy and the book drops to her side as she falls asleep.

Her body became slack in his arms. He supported her against him, bracing himself against the car, trying not to disturb her flood of memories. Her breathing deepened, as if she had lost consciousness, but he could see that her eyes were still wide open as she stared hypnotically at the tree.

"Frances?" His voice travelled through a fog of time. "Where are you?"

"I've been asleep," she said yawning.

"In the tree?"

Fugue

She wakes in the dark to the sound of rain and thunder and lightning. Wind moans through the leaves of the tree, rising gradually to a shrieking wail.

"So wet!" she whimpered in fear. Her chest heaved with jerky breaths.
"What?"

She peers below her hiding place to see two young men who are drinking beer and throwing the bottles at the trunk, laughing drunkenly. She can smell the beer from where she is hiding. She is alarmed and tries to escape down the other side of the tree but falls.

Frances screamed in pain. "My leg!"

The men hear her and she hides inside the roots that lead into dark wet caverns. She can hear them looking for her as they stumble, laughing, around the tree. The walls of her hiding place are tall enough to remain hidden where she stands shaking with cold. Rough hands seek her out and pull her from her hiding place. She is on the ground looking up at the huge fig tree looming monstrous in the heavy downpour, wide branches curve furtively over their ghostly twisted roots. The faces of the men alternately blot out the tree as they violate her body. She screams and screams as she is ripped into two. And they laugh as they force beer into her screaming, choking mouth.

"It hurts. Oh, it hurts! Stop! Please stop!"

Her vision is slammed from side to side as open hands slap her face. She sees rain fill the puddles on the ground beside her, then a sweeping view of the tree as her head slams in the opposite direction, rain and puddles near the men's car on the other side. Back to the tree, the ground, the tree, the ground,

186

the tree, the ground. Faster. Faster. Screaming. Tearing. Choking. Slapping. Rain washing beer from her face. Mud. Screaming.

"Noooo! Noooo! Someone! Help me! Noooo! Mummy…"

Hands. Gentle hands. They turned her around and she saw an indistinct but worried face replacing that of the men who had leered into her innocent face and body. This was a face she could cling to. A face that had tears to match her own. A face that looked at her with love and compassion and understanding. This was a face she could not let go of.

The roaring of the wind and rain and loathsome laughter crept from her mind until it faded and there was silence. The last thing she felt was the splashing of Adam's tears on her face as he bent closer, and she relinquished her brittle hold upon the world to tumble into blissful, welcoming oblivion.

Chapter 22

The droning of the aircraft's engines had lulled them into a peaceful quietude as they sat waiting for their journey to end. Frances leaned her face against the window, staring out, while Adam rested his head against the back of his seat, his eyes closed, lost deep in thought.

It had been an anxious time for him during Frances's reliving of her childhood trauma. He wondered if he had gone too far—forcing her to face the memory of the rape—when she had fainted in his arms. He berated himself for attempting something that perhaps should have been left to a psychiatrist and fervently hoped that he hadn't caused any further damage to her tortured mind.

When she'd revived, he'd helped her into the back seat of the car and had sat with her, holding her, wondering where he could find the closest doctor. He would have to take her to one, he decided, so that she could be given something to calm her. Or perhaps even a hospital. He certainly wouldn't take her back to her father's house. The man had forfeited any claim upon his daughter as far as Adam was concerned. *Would he care anyway?*

A passionate feeling of wanting to protect her swept over him, not for the first time, and he vowed to himself, if she would let him, to make up for all the hurt and rejection she had suffered.

At last the enigma of her past was revealed, not only to him but, more importantly, to herself. Would this be a healing revelation? Something that would allow her to get on with and participate in life? A revelation that would permit her to put the past aside and turn her face to the future?

As he studied the trees lining the road, he felt her stir. She looked up at him.

He smiled. "Are you all right?"

"I…think so." She sat up. She looked out of the window at the fig tree, then back at him, shaking her head. "I've put you through so much," she whispered.

"I think it's the other way around," he grimaced.

Her breath came out in a shudder. "It was awful."

"I can only imagine."

She closed her eyes for a moment then sighed as she looked at him again.

"Are you okay to travel now?" he asked her.

"Where…?"

"To a doctor. I think you need some attention."

Her head shook from side to side. "No. No doctor." Reluctant to break the contact with the protection of his body, she leaned back against him. His arms went instinctively around her.

"But…"

"They can't do anything. Not now."

"Well, if you're sure…" he said, loosening his hold around her.

"Can we…can we stay here just a bit longer?"

A flight attendant leaned across Adam with a tray of food, the movement interrupting his thoughts. He saw that Frances had already put the shelf down from the back of the seat in front of her and she put the tray upon it without interest. Adam undid the latch to release his shelf and the flight attendant placed his tray on it with a smile.

"Would you like a drink?" she asked.

Frances shook her head.

Adam said, "No. Nothing for either of us, thanks."

Neither of them attempted to unwrap the food from its foil packaging, and remained staring at the crammed trays for a long moment.

Eventually Adam said quietly, "Who were they?"

"I don't know." Frances shuddered. Her voice became child-like as she asked, "Why did they hurt me?"

Adam shook his head, tears filling his eyes. He cleared his throat. "What did your parents do?"

"They never knew."

"What?"

"They were away." She paused as the memories flooded back. "And those men…they told me they would kill me…and my parents…if I told anyone."

"The servants?"

She shook her head. "I told no one. I thought my parents—everyone—would hate me for the rest of my life! I felt so dirty!"

"And you shut it out all these years?"

"Yes."

"How old were you?"

"Ten."

Disturbing images of the physical damage, the pain she must have suffered, flashed through his mind. *And she faced it alone.*

They paused outside the Queen Victoria Women's Centre, a heritage-listed Edwardian Baroque tower in Lonsdale Street. The ornate grey portico, that headed two short flights of steps, had a feeling of permanency, solidity and shelter.

"This must be it," Adam said, giving Frances's arm a slight squeeze.

She looked down at her scribbled notes: *CASA House, 3ʳᵈ floor.* She mouthed silently, *Centre Against Sexual Assault.*

"You still want me to wait outside?" he asked.

Frances touched him on the arm. "Yes. I have to do this myself…finally."

"I'll be waiting." His fingers brushed her hand lightly.

"I know." She returned his touch, then climbed the steps, turned to look at Adam briefly, and continued through the entrance.

He leaned against the exterior fencing, thinking about how far she'd come. This was such a positive and important step in her recovery. Traffic blundered along the road, heedless of the human traumas, both mental and physical, that were being addressed on both sides of the street. At least here, he felt, she would be understood and hopefully healed.

Samuel shuffled in his usual seat beside Frances in the front row of the stalls in Hamer Hall. Adam entered the stage to the applause of the audience, and he bowed acknowledging their welcome. He smiled down at Frances who smiled back at him, most traces of shyness or reticence now disappeared.

The gentle passion of the *Meditation* from *Thais* lifted Frances into the orchestration so that she was aware only of Adam's fluid movements as he and the other musicians interpreted Massenet's score. The lilting suspension of the perfect notes floated through the hall, embracing the ears with a caress that melted the sternest heart.

And so Samuel observed his companion seated beside him, her profile radiating a happiness that he had never seen before. There was a sense of peace about her, yet a sense of expectancy. He saw that she was lost in the music and the man she was looking at. Tears were not a part of this moment.

From the opening with its serene motif, Samuel was transported, as always in the *Meditation,* to a mental image of gentle waves lapping a quiet seashore. The violin entered like a calm breeze, gradually growing stronger, yet remaining gracious, before the melody passed unbroken into a forceful theme. It seemed to him to represent the conflict between good and evil—the agonizing decision that Thais had to make between one life and the other—which reflected the transition between Frances's old life and the new one that Adam offered her. But the theme's conflict was fleeting and the ethereal mood dominated again. He sighed quietly and contentedly as a serenity washed over him, the *Meditation* near its end. The forceful theme returned, implying an optimistic outcome rather than one of menace.

The last long single perfect note that rose from Adam's violin left the hall momentarily hushed before the audience broke into rapturous applause. Unable to resist, Samuel took Frances's hand in his, squeezing it gently. She turned to look at him, her eyes shining. *God, she's so happy!* He lifted her hand to his lips and kissed it gently, signalling his approval. Her smile was dazzling as she read his thoughts in his eyes. He let go and she turned back to the stage taking in a long deep breath as her gaze returned to Adam.

Samuel looked at the man who had not, after all, taken her from him. Adam had returned her, a woman who could give friendship and companionship unreservedly, a woman who would now submerge herself in life.

And Samuel loved that man.

Epilogue – Two Years Later

Frances pushed her hair back as she gazed out at the gardens. "Doesn't it look particularly beautiful today? Especially after last night's rain."

"It does," Gail nodded, as she looked up from her plate. "It needed a good drink. Such a relief from the heat, isn't it?"

"Oh, yes," Frances breathed. "Thank goodness for airconditioning. I've hardly moved from home these past days. I feel like I'm melting."

Gail regarded her friend. "You still look as cool as a cucumber, you know. Despite what you're carrying."

"I don't feel cool," Frances grimaced, unconsciously putting a hand to her stomach.

"Maybe she's been waiting for the heatwave to finish before making her grand entrance."

"Well, she'll have to make up her mind soon or she'll miss her father's world premiere."

"At least it's going to be simulcast on the ABC, so both of you can listen to it from your room…unless you're busy huffing and puffing! You won't miss a thing, except," Gail grinned, "seeing that gorgeous hunk of yours on stage before his adoring audience."

"Well," Frances smiled, "we've got two weeks until the performance, and my doctor says any day now. She told me she's laying bets it'll be on Friday."

"Cutting it fine, isn't it?"

"Yes, it is," Frances agreed, "but what can we do? He can't postpone the performance."

"Fingers crossed, then."

"You know, it's such a milestone for him. Every time I hear it, I can't believe how beautiful it is. Living with a mind so creative and stunning is a bit mind blowing."

"Ahh," Gail sighed as she sipped her wine, "brains as well as beauty. I can't believe I know a talented violinist who's also a composer. Of a whole violin concerto!" She held up her glass. "To your handsome, magnificent, loveable husband."

"If I didn't know any better, I'd swear you were jealous."

"Of course I'm jealous," Gail exclaimed, "Insanely jealous. I'd give my eye teeth – and that's saying something – for a man like Adam."

"But Dennis…"

"Dennis is a lovely lovely man but, hey, he can't exactly woo me with a violin stick – sorry, bow – and his teeth aren't a patch on Adam's, though I'm working on his even though he tests my patience trying to talk when I'm in there…"

"But…"

"I know. I know," Gail held up her hands in surrender. "I know you say I talk all the time and you can't answer, but I swear Dennis just won't shut up. I keep telling him to save it. I'm terrified I'm going to split his tongue with the drill." She laughed at Frances's horrified look. "Just joking."

"Well, that's a relief," Frances laughed with her. "I was considering changing my dentist."

"Over my dead body. Your teeth are mine!"

"Well, since I have them on loan for our lunch, I think I'll make use of them," Frances said, lifting a prawn to her mouth.

"I saw that!" Adam laughed, placing his hand on Frances's stomach. "Go on, do it again," he urged his unborn child. "Say hi to your father now that he's home from work." An energetic kick met his hand. "See," he said, "she can hear me!"

"You're still determined it'll be a girl!" Frances said, shaking her head. "Will you be awfully disappointed if it's a boy?"

"Of course not," he smiled. "It's just that I'd love to have a girl first – a mirror of you. But if a boy it is, then he'll still look like you…"

"Oh, no," she laughed, 'he'll be the spitting imagine of his father. Imagine when he grows up playing the violin, on stage with you. Playing a concerto for two violins that you've written. Now, that'd be something, eh?"

"You know, I'm so fortunate to have a wife who believes in me. Who loves me for who and what I am. But, in the meantime," he said, "she or he had better look the other way because Daddy's going to kiss Mummy in a most decadent way."

Frances caught her breath as he gazed into her eyes, her lips tingling with anticipation. Slowly, ever so slowly, he lowered his lips to hers, with a touch so light it was as if a breeze played across them, yet with the force of an electric current that travelled over and under her chin, glanced down her neck and into her breast. She gasped as his kiss intensified, hungry for him to continue, wanting him, wanting every part of him.

Not for the first time did she wonder at the feelings and sensations he could coax from her mind and body. He'd waited, with a patience that must have been agony, for her to begin healing. He'd slowly peeled the layers from her cocoon, as the gruelling counselling had laid bare her trauma.

And yet, when her father took his life six months after her mother died, her recovery seemed to take a step forward as she shed the shackles of her childhood. And the nightmares ceased.

Frances tiptoed into an intimate relationship hesitantly and fearfully as Adam guided her onto a path she could trust.

How can he give me so much of himself and stay sane, she asked herself many times. *Because he loves me.* "How can I be so lucky," she mumbled against his lips. "How can…?"

"I love you. That's all that matters. And that makes me very lucky too."

Her mobile suddenly demanded attention, pulling them apart.

"It's Samuel," Frances smiled, as she picked up her mobile.

"Hello there! Is that my favourite bookshop calling?"

She stifled a giggle as Adam nuzzled her neck.

"Yes, yes. Seven o'clock. I hope Philip likes seafood?"

www.ingramcontent.com/pod-product-compliance
Lightning Source LLC
Chambersburg PA
CBHW050329110726
47899CB00007B/2424